OTHER BOOKS

Anthology of Aussie romance stories

CHARMS of LOVE

FOREWORD BY GINA PINTO

Copyright ©2024 Charms of Love

FIRST EDITION: 2024

978-0-9756535-1-7 (pbk)
978-0-975635-2-4 (ebk)

The moral right of the author has been asserted.
Foreword © Gina Pinto
ROMANTASY AND SPECULATIVE ROMANCE
Splashes of Blood © R. A. Purtill
Perfect Man © Rita Maclean
Butterfly © Gary David
Bruce © Robin Martin Thomas
The Guest Room © Sarah Hegerty
Eye of the Storm © Jeanette O'Hagan

CONTEMPORARY ROMANCE
Within the Fire © Robin Adolphs
The Wilderness Cure © Lea Scott
Floyd Jackson is Dead © Emma Rennison
Spruzzi d'amore © Jenny Woolsey
The Boy with the Kaleidoscope Eyes © Lily Mulholland
Tahitian Jewel © Elizabeth Spratt
Sleepover © Aura Gold
Going the Distance © Kate Kelsen

Cover layout by Charmaine Clancy
Lead editor and interior layout by Christine Titheradge

Interior edit by Gina Pinto
Interior support by Self-Publishing Lab

CONTENTS

FOREWORD

On a retreat with windows framing the pristine rainforest and the presenters offering inspiration on tap, I discovered the endless possibilities within a love story. It is filled with countless meet-cute moments, guilty pleasures, blushing protagonists, and happy-ever-after endings. The Rainforest Writers Retreat (RWR) opened the imagination and passion of its writers to tackle the best-selling genre—Romance.

This anthology will satiate readers of Contemporary Romance with a poem that ignites the heart, music-magic at a festival, prince charming scenarios, eco-themed love, Italian to Tahitian infused romances, and the bittersweet tale of a long-distance relationship. This collection not only showcases the breadth of talent at RWR, but also offers fans of Speculative fiction with romances entangled in fantasy, Gothicism, Virtual Reality, and artificial intelligence. It also includes the sub-genres surfacing out of Contemporary—from Inspirational to Celebrity Romance.

There is no one way into Romance and each writer opened a window to their romantic side to shine a light on the genre and its many different types of happy endings.

Wherever you may be, enjoy *Charms of Love* created with love by the retreaters at RWR.

—Gina Pinto

ROMANTASY

AND

SPECULATIVE

ROMANCE

SPLASHES OF BLOOD

r. a. purtill

The night I sucked on my finger to soothe a wound was the night I fell in love.

I removed my hand from my mouth, and holding it above the kitchen sink, I squeezed until dark red drips joined the swirling, watery dance.

'Goodness, girl. You need to be more careful.' Mum peered over my shoulder. 'Why aren't you wearing gloves?'

'It isn't even my turn. Where's Ada?'

'She has a date. You can swap tomorrow.' She let out the plug and refreshed the water.

'Why can't we have a dishwasher?' I asked.

'You know how your father feels about technology.'

I rolled my eyes. 'I swear he thinks we're still living in the Middle Ages.'

'Have you finished your essay?' Mum punctuated the change of topic with a clang of cutlery into the drainer.

I shrugged. 'I've got the weekend. Who's she out with, anyway?'

'I think she said his name was Bradley Farmer. Some kind of journalist.'

'She's at it again, isn't she? Luring some unsuspecting creature—'

'If she thought he was a creature of the night, I am sure she wouldn't put herself in danger.'

I scoffed, 'It's not Ada who's in danger.'

'Do you need that cut tended to?' Mum changed the subject again.

The bleeding had stopped, and a throbbing red line now decorated the side of my index finger.

'Nah. It will be okay. I'll be in my room.'

Later that night, headlights made patterns on the bedroom ceiling as a vehicle rolled into the driveway. I stood and watched Ada and her date sitting in the front seat. And that's when it happened. He glanced up at me and waved. I pressed my hand to the bedroom window in response. Since I became aware of Ada's tactic of choice, luring the unsuspecting enemy on dates to gain their trust like some black widow spider, I had been waiting for the one that I would save from her hunting instincts.

Bradley Farmer's hair appeared silver in the surrounding lights of the street and the house. When he and Ada emerged, his tall frame reached the front door in three strides. My elder sister may have a dark fate designed for him, but I now had another destiny in mind: this was the one I had to save.

I tiptoed into the corridor and strained to hear their conversation. His low voice was smooth and sincere. Whatever he said made Ada giggle. Then the kissing noises started, and I made my move.

'Don't mind me,' I said, bumping Brad's leg.

They stopped and stood awkwardly as I passed on my way to the kitchen. Behind me I knew Ada had daggers for eyes. *Let her.* I had just one goal now.

When I returned with a mug of chocolate milk, I made sure I locked eyes with Brad. I thought I would be the strong one in this exchange but found myself unstable under his bright dark eyes. I tripped and the contents of my mug splashed across Ada's white blouse. Her squeal brought Mum and Dad from the living room.

'This is Bradley Farmer,' I announced.

The daggers in Ada's eyes flew at me. 'I hate you.'

Then I recognised the understanding that passed between Ada and Dad. So, they were in this one together. I was right about Bradley Farmer. I had to rescue him no matter what.

Ada took Brad's arm and led him out the front door.

I watched from the window while they said a brief goodbye filled with promises I knew Ada would never keep. When she returned inside and went upstairs, I joined him by the car.

'Lydia, isn't it?'

Oh, the way he said my name. The way it fell from his tongue. The blood rushed to my face, pounded round my head.

3

I scanned him but sensed nothing. Perhaps my senses were already overloaded by him and couldn't take in more. Perhaps he was the devious one and could hide his true nature? Or perhaps he was innocent after all, and I was about to sabotage a genuine date that had nothing to do with Ada's nefarious trap.

'How does a journalist afford a Beamer?' I asked.

'Who told you I was a journalist?'

'Mum said.' I walked around the vehicle but really, I was inspecting him. Solid build, neatly trimmed, the warm smell of the engine ...

'I'm a novelist,' he said. 'Perhaps your sister was covering for me to impress your parents. At least *journalist* sounds like I have a job.' He smiled and fiddled with his car keys as we stood beside the driver's door.

'What are you writing?'

'Research. Local supernatural history. I spend my days in the library.'

I made a mental note of that information. He sniffed the air. 'Is that your perfume?'

I shrugged. 'Just a splash.'

'It's nice. I really must go.'

I took my time stepping back to let him in the car. He had to slide past my shoulder to get in. When he brushed my arm against his, my senses bristled to attention. He was what Ada knew him to be. *You can be safe with me. I am not like them.*

He caught my gaze for a moment as though he had heard my thoughts, then simply said, 'Bye,' before pulling the door shut.

I stood in the driveway until the red taillights turned left at the T-junction.

Bradley Farmer didn't respond to any of Ada's calls after that night and she became sullen and unbearable. I was too busy to care. I was on a mission. All through that week, the garage became my happy place. I soon had an impressive collection of articles, newspaper clippings, photographs, maps, and journals about the otherworldly history of the town. As I gathered it, I imagined how appreciative Brad would be and I blushed. On the Saturday morning, I stacked my offerings in a trolley and set out for the library. Dad was in the front yard pruning trees.

'What have you got there, love?'

'Oh, a family history project for college.' It felt like a betrayal of family secrets, but if it meant Brad would live, it had to be.

He raised an eyebrow and peered in. 'Are you sure you have enough?'

'I couldn't decide, so I thought I'd just take it all.' I waved a hand over the contents of the trolley. 'It's okay, isn't it? You always say we should keep to ourselves.'

He looked at me in earnest. 'I trust you to be discerning in what you share. It's good to see you're finally taking an interest in our ancient cause. Don't be late for dinner.' He patted my shoulder and returned to his trees.

The little bell above the door pinged as I entered the library backwards, pulling the trolley up the stairs with both hands. A girl in a council uniform held the door and I asked, 'Do you know where I can find Bradley Farmer?'

'Mystery, left back corner.'

'Not his books,' I laughed at the misunderstanding. 'He told me he'd be here.'

'He is. In the Mystery section, left back corner. As I said.' She glared at me then turned on her officious heels muttering something about how nobody listens anymore. I wheeled my way down to a table and chair by the window.

'Well, hello Lydia. What's all this?'

I caught my breath. 'It's for your research.'

'For me?' When he smiled, I knew I had done the right thing.

I joined him at the table, spread out the contents of my trolley and with our heads close together we poured over the treasure. He didn't even mention Ada once the whole time.

'This is your family?' he asked. I could feel the awe in his voice. 'And they have always lived here?'

I nodded and ran my injured finger along a contour as if the line on my hand and the lines on the map were connected somehow. When Brad took my wrist and lifted it away, a shiver ran through me. His cool skin covered my wound as he held my hand longer than necessary. When our eyes met, our souls became tethered. Hunter and hunted shouldn't find love, but we did. With our hands folded together we turned to the map before us on the table.

'I think these are ley lines,' he said. 'Look. Here is the graveyard on Thompson Street and this alignment runs straight to ...' He stepped back and stared at me. 'Your place.'

'Oh?' I pretended I didn't understand.

He folded his arms and said, 'You knew, didn't you?'

'Sort of, but no one has ever really explained it. We just keep secrets all the time. And when I thought you were interested, I just had to ...'

He put his hand on my shoulder. 'It's okay. I'm glad you did. This stuff is gold.' He glanced at his watch.

'I've got to go. Can you meet me tonight around eight?'

'Sure.'

'I'll pick you up at the T-junction.' He collected his coat, glanced one last time at the table, and then picked up a leather-bound journal. 'Mind if I take this?'

When I nodded, he slid it into his satchel and gave my arm a final squeeze.

'See you tonight,' he said, and disappeared behind a nearby bookshelf.

As I trundled home, his words became the rhythm of the trolley wheels. 'Meet me tonight. See you tonight. Meet me tonight.'

By the time I entered the house, I was humming with happiness. Ada scowled and spoke to me for the first time since I crashed her 'date'.

'What's with you? You look like you have a crush.'

'It's not a crush. It's real.' I left her with that and escaped to my room.

Sneaking out later was easier than I expected. Ada was finally doing her turn at dishes while Mum and Dad shared the newspaper at the kitchen table. I slipped out the front door unnoticed.

I hadn't been waiting long when the black BMW cruised down the road and stopped by me. I slid in beside Brad and we pulled away from the curb.

'Are we going to the graveyard?' I asked.

'Yup,' he said, not taking his eyes off the road.

In the tray under the glovebox in front of me was the leather journal he had taken that morning.

'Find anything in this?' I asked.

The yellow pages were full of diagrams and indecipherable handwritten notes. I had given up trying to understand it before, but now I flipped through it curious as to why Brad had chosen it out of the collection I had given him. There was a smaller version of the map we had seen with the ley lines, and on the lower corner of one page was an anatomical drawing of a man. I flicked the page. It was an animation, each corner the next iteration of a transformation. The final movement revealed a creature of the night with long incisors dripping with blood and an unconscious body in its arms. I tossed the journal back in the tray as though I'd been burned.

'That's what you're researching?'

'Scary stuff, heh, but it makes great reading. Well, it will when I finish it.' He grinned at me sideways.

'I prefer a good romance.'

'You might have to settle for a bad one.' He laughed at his joke, then his expression softened, and his smile touched the nerves in my stomach.

When we arrived at the graveyard, he turned off the engine and leant over to me until our faces were close and I could feel his body vibrate with expectation.

'May I?'

When I agreed, he planted his teeth hard under my ear, sucking until my life was drawn up to his mouth. In the rear-view mirror, I saw a blotchy splash of love flower like a medallion on my neck. Then he searched for my lips, pushed them open and found his way in. We kissed for ages like that. When we pulled apart, he frowned at me and appeared disappointed.

'You didn't change?' he said.

What did he know? I was completely changed. Nothing would ever be the same again.

'Everything is changed,' I whispered.

'You didn't become like me.'

I shook my head. 'No. You cannot turn me. We are immortal and ancient. And we're dangerous to you. Oh, Brad, I am so sorry. You're caught up in something you can't possibly understand.'

'I know more than you think.'

'I guess all your research helped, but—'

From the pocket of his denim shirt, he took out a leather band and placed it into my palm.

'I always wear it. Hunters are everywhere,' he said.

'Brad ... you need to know ... that ... we ... I ...'

We stared at each other in silence. I watched the realisation arrive on his beautiful face and said, 'You need to take this back. You're still in danger.'

'Your family?'

9

'I had to save you from them.'

Brad's amulet of protection fell to the floor of the car and was lost when headlights lit us up like the day and the sound of crunching gravel brought a car to a halt in front of us. We jumped from the car. I grabbed Brad's hand and was ready to run.

'Get away from him, Lydia.' The owner of the voice was obscured but I recognised him.

'Dad.'

Brad and I froze.

'Come to me, darling.' *Mum too?*

I didn't move from Brad's side.

'He's a vampire.' Dad stepped out of the blinding light and came toward us.

'And I am going to save him from you.' I stood directly in front of Brad with my arms out, making myself the target, as if my small body could ever cover his tall frame.

'No, Lydia, don't do this,' said Brad.

'I'll do whatever it takes.'

He ran his fingers around the mark he'd made on my neck and silently shook his head.

I was frantic. 'We have to be together.'

Mum's desperation mirrored my own. 'Lydia, please. Move before—

And then it happened. Brad groaned and convulsed behind me. I turned to see his face drain of colour. He fell forward and crashed into my arms. Beyond his quivering shoulder, Ada lowered her crossbow. Her trap had snared us both. She came to Brad's truck, retrieved the journal, and held it up in triumph.

I dropped to the ground holding Brad as he struggled for life.

Everything was blurred, in my head, in my vision as the tears came. 'Don't leave me.'

'Llll ...'

'Yes, I'm here.'

His arm was stretched out on the dark earth. When I reached to bring it closer to me, I realised Brad had been pointing to the ground.

'Llll ...' he repeated.

In a moment all was clear. Ley lines! Of course. If he died on a ley line, there might be a chance.

'You'll have to help me,' I said, sliding out from under him.

Mum and Dad closed in, whether to finish him off, or to rescue me, I wasn't sure.

'Stop. Don't do it,' Dad called.

I lifted Brad's shoulders and heaved, dragging him the few feet to where the ley line glowed. An arrow zinged passed my head.

'First warning, sister,' said Ada.

Brad rolled on to his side and crawled on one elbow toward the line, groaning with each movement. Another arrow whizzed into the ground. I ducked and rolled onto the ley line with my arms out ready to receive Brad. One final grunt and he dove into me. We lay panting and crying and then Ada was above us on one side and Dad and Mum arrived on the other. I looked up at my family. Were they really going to destroy us?

Another arrow. This time the sound was cut short with a thud as it speared Brad's body and through to the ground. His life splashed out like bloody vampire vomit.

'Nooo. How could you?' I grabbed the arrow and began to heave but the tearing of flesh and the cracking of bone stopped me.

'Let's go. We're done here,' said Ada.

Dad followed her, but Mum stayed. I pushed her arm away when she tried to touch me.

'Come on Lydia. You got to the line too late,' she said. 'Let's go.'

I shook my head and dropped on my knees beside Brad.

'I'll wait for you in the car,' Mum finally said and walked away.

I wished I was cold and dead like him, but I was alive even though all life had been taken from me. It was near dawn when the mist rose, and the barest of red sunrise lit the grey clouds. Something stirred beneath me. In the rising light, Brad's eyes fluttered open.

All the capillaries in my body tingled. I ran my hand through the grass around him and felt the power fade from there. I held him tight and sobbed.

'The ley line saved you!'

'You saved me,' he said, his breath warm on my neck.

'Now we can be together forever, can't we?'

He kissed me lightly as he held my tear smudged face. Then his soft hands darkened, and a black leather membrane grew from his forearms. He drew it around us both. With his face close to mine, he whispered, 'Find me.'

'Wait. What?'

The dark canopy lifted away from me and against the flaming sky, a large bat circled the air above the ley line and escaped the coming light.

'Find me,' he said, and so I went searching. I knew each ley line from point to point. I studied every page in that journal once Ada gave it up and I endured my sister's taunts as she gloated over her subsequent victories. On those nights when the moon was new, obscured in the sky because it reflected no light, I was destined to join the hunt with my family. But unlike my elder sister and my parents, I did not hunt to destroy. I hunted to love.

One evening, I was at our backyard fence where the ley lines begin. Within the grass the lines glowed like a row of candles on an airport runway, as if they were guiding in the next flight. With a whoosh and the sound of wings retracting, Brad appeared, standing before me as a human guardian of the night. I leapt the fence and rushed to him. At our reunion the planets came into alignment.

And so it is, each new moon night, for a few sweet hours, until the colours of the dawn splash through the trees, we are together.

PERFECT MAN

rita maclean

He was walking further up the beach. She saw him drop the stone. And so, it began—she hoped. She picked up the stone and held her breath. Rubbing its smooth heart shape as she stared out to sea pretending not to be waiting for him.

'You're holding my heart in your hands,' said his warm caramel voice.

'It's not the first time I've held someone's heart.' She chuckled and handed back the heart-stone.

'That sounds like an interesting conversation. Maybe we could talk over coffee?' He held out his hand. 'I'm Josef.'

'Coffee would be great.' She took his hand. 'I'm Mirri.'

'I didn't see a coffee shop in town,' said Josef.

'The coffee shop went out of business.' Mirri smiles, relieved to hear Josef recalling memories of the town. 'I have coffee facilities at my B&B.'

'I didn't see a B&B.'

'My place isn't in town.' Good, he's remembering more details. 'It's in the rainforest. Very secluded.'

'It's my lucky day.' Josef looked meekly down at the fizzing waves rolling across their feet. 'Or it could be, if you have a spare room available.'

'Where have you been staying?'

'I slept on the beach. I haven't found anywhere to stay in town, and I thought—but if you don't—'

'I have a room for you. It'll be dusty, but you're welcome to it.'

'Great.'

'It's this way.' They turned and strolled together up the beach. Mirri pondering what she should tell him.

'Nice area. Guests must love it out here,' said Josef.

'It's beautiful, but the B&B isn't much of a going concern because I get too distracted with my research to have guests.'

'Research?'

'Science nerd.' Mirri raised her hands. 'Guilty as charged.'

'What are you researching?'

'Telomeres and cellular reconstruction.' She squinted a smile at him. 'We turn here.'

A tilted woodworm eaten sign pointed into a cool corridor of green at the edge of the beach. Mirri led the way as the path twisted and turned through a moist tangle of green. The rainforest thinned to reveal a gap-toothed wooden fence. She rested her hand on the gate latch, hesitating.

'Can you do me a favour?' said asked

'Sure.'

She pulled a small pouch from her pocket and took out some cash. 'Can you go to town and grab some food: fish, meat, cheese, some wine. Choose what you like.' She gestured to take his backpack. He shrugged it off. 'It'll give me time to tidy things away, so you feel ... more at home.' She gazed off for a moment then laughed a little. 'I wouldn't want to shock you with all my secrets.' She handed him the cash and pointed to a less trodden track. 'That's a short-cut.'

Watching as he walked away, she sighed. *It's a good idea him going into town.* She unlatched the gate. *When he tells people he's new to the area and he slept on the beach. Then he met me and is staying at the B&B.* She shoved the gate open. *That story will convince everyone.*

Following the narrow path to the far corner of the garden, Mirri stopped, laying her hand on top of the warm cairn of stones that was her father's grave. Then she twisted through the lush kitchen garden, stepped up and walked along the wide wooden verandah. She entered her cluttered lab, and focused on putting samples and equipment away. She closed her notebooks and journals and stacked them neatly. Stopping to scan the lab, she stepped into the cold-room.

Turning in a slow circle, she looked at the history of her project, the work she'd done with her father before he'd died. Before she'd failed to use the science of her project to save him. Mirri gently, touched the limbs laying in shallow tubs, gazed at the skin and organs floating half formed in jars. All of which had been *appropriated* or cultured, and all of them told the story

17

of the project and the potential of that work to save and change lives — if, and when it could be accepted by those who needed it.

That acceptance, she knew was a long way off, but the next couple of weeks would give insight into the success of her work and the chances of any type of acceptance. Shivering, she stepped out of the cold room and locked it. Then walked out onto the verandah and locked the lab door.

Halfway through a cursory dusting of the guest room, she heard whistling. Josef was strolling through the garden with a box of supplies and a huge smile. She loved that smile.

'Is all that tidying up for me?' He put the box down on a round wooden table on the verandah.

'Sure is. I'm being a good host. I want you to feel at home.'

'I appreciate it.' Josef looked around at the timber house and the gardens surrounded by walls of rainforest green. 'This place is amazing. Did you build it?'

'My father built it years ago. I inherited it when he died ... a while back.'

'He built a lab for you.' He pointed at the locked door. 'Is it in there?'

'Yeah, and he built the lab for himself.' She smiled reminiscing about the work she'd done alongside her father. 'I also inherited the science nerd thing from him.' She locked eyes with Josef, she could see more in those eyes than had been there before. His skin shined, sweaty from the effort of carrying the supplies through the humid morning. 'Thanks for getting these.' She took the box from the table. 'I'll get you a drink.'

Mirri made the excuse of being between projects to keep the lab closed and keep her attention on Josef. For a few days, they lounged and chatted, dug and harvested in the garden. She asked about his life, teasing out his memories when and how it seemed appropriate.

Fish and vegies roasted in the oven on the end of the verandah. The evening breeze and the wine had made them lazy and comfortable.

'What's your favourite place in the world?' she asked.

'Apart from here,' he smiled.

'I'm flattered, but yes.'

'New Zealand, north island, it's all lush plants and trembling earth.'

'You should be a travel writer.'

'I could be. I've wandered all over the place.' He sipped his wine. 'Where's your favourite?'

'Iceland, the auroras.'

'I agree. I loved watching the plasma bounce off the atmosphere.' Mirri sipped and nodded, pleased with the consistency of these recollections.

'This place is beautiful, but it's miles from nowhere.' Josef pressed his lips closed as though doubting his next words. 'Why here? Why not somewhere closer to colleagues and ... I don't know, science stuff?'

'Dad and I worked on a very experimental concept. Seeking funding was difficult, so it was easier to go independent with the project.'

'That sounds costly.'

'Less than you might think. Dad had sold his house for a big profit, then bought this place and built the lab.' Mirri stared at her wine for a moment. 'The day they announced my research grant wasn't being renewed, was the day Dad told me he was sick. I sold my place in the city and shipped everything I could acquire from my old lab to here.'

'I didn't mean to open all that up for you.' Josef squeezed her hand.

'That's fine. It was great working with Dad and we were so close to curing him, until we weren't. But he made me promise to stay true to the project.' Mirri squeezed Josef's hand. 'Dad was right, of course. His postmortem gave me the answers ... the ironic eureka moment.'

'Some good came from his loss then.' Josef fidgeted, standing and reaching to refill their glasses.

'I'm still experimenting, but I hope good things will come of it. New science can be very hard to accept.'

Josef held her hand to steady her glass as he poured. She trembled again. He spilt wine on both their hands. 'Sorry.' He put the bottle down and took her glass.

'It's okay.' She smiled, placing her lips to the trickle of wine on the back of his hand. 'I'm done with science and wine for a while.' She ran her hands up Josef's arm, his neck. Leaning in, she tasted the wine on his lips. She wondered if the kiss was happening because of emotions or the experiment. Josef wrapped his arms around her and it was all about the kiss.

Josef was shirtless, digging up sweet potato. She watched the muscles in his back working, strong and flexible. Her eyes traced the barely visible lines that swept arcs across his tanned shoulders. His appearance pleased her on many levels. When she found herself thinking of the touch of his warm skin, she shook her head to break the spell.

'It looks like you really know what you're doing with the garden,' she said, wanting to delve deeper into Josef's past and share his reminiscences—experimenting again.

'It comes naturally to me. I've always had a knack for this type of work.' His eyes dropped as he looked into his memories. Mirri held her breath a moment.

'I've always been pretty restless,' he continued. 'I've moved around a lot with work.'

'Well, you have an impressive depth of knowledge with the plants.' She walked over inhaling his sun-warmed scent as she held out a flask of cool water.

'Thanks,' he said. Taking off his garden gloves and taking the bottle he drank slowly. 'There's not much else about me that's deep.' He gave a weak laugh. 'I've travelled and worked and learnt a lot, but the restlessness isn't great for friendships or relationships.'

'So, there's no one special you'd give your heart-stone to?'

'No one memorable. Same with friends, they come and go with each job.' Mirri nodded, pleased about what she was learning from these glimpses of memory.

'What about family?'

'I'm going to sound like I've just walked out of a country song, but here we go. My parents died when I was young. I was raised by my great-aunt. She was wonderful, and old. She's gone now.'

'What's your favourite memory about her?' Mirri watched Josef, listening intently.

'Tomato relish.' He smiled.

'Okay.'

'She had a huge garden, a bit like this, and there were always too many tomatoes so we'd make relish.' He sighed. 'She'd sell it at her old lady club and then she'd give me all the profits.'

'How wonderful.' Mirri felt very satisfied to hear that memory.

Josef placed his hand on Mirri's shoulder and trailed his gentle fingers up to the curve of her neck. Her breath shuddered. He hesitated then kissed her. His lips cool from the water then suddenly hot. His hand slid up her neck, his fingers tangling into her hair.

Leaning into the kiss, Mirri wrapped her arms around Josef's back. She traced the lines encircling each shoulder blade, the lines were so fine you wouldn't feel them unless you knew they were there.

The water bottle thudded to the ground and Josef's other hand was on her waste, then moving, feather light up her spine, then down to her hip. He pulled her in close, so close.

As she led him through the garden to the shaded daybed on the verandah. Ideas of experiments and innovations were washed away like sand on the beach.

The late-afternoon breeze chilled Mirri's bare skin and she shivered awake. Josef lay next to her watching her and smiling. He swept the tangled hair off her face and kissed her. Then rolled off the daybed tied a sarong around his hips and poured them some wine. Mirri tied her own sarong and moved to sit in the last patch of afternoon sun. Josef sat beside her and offered the glass without speaking.

'Thanks.' She felt suddenly awkward and guessed Josef felt the same. 'You okay?' she ventured.

'I'm envious.' He stared at the setting sun refracting through his wine glass.

'Of what?'

'Of you. Of this place.' The wine splashed as he twisted the glass around to catch the sun again. 'You have this place and your work. This may sound weird. I know it's only been a short while, but I feel a deep connection here.'

Mirri's smile broadened. 'Not weird, and I'm flattered. I must be doing something right if that's how you're feeling.' She lifted her glass. 'Here's to finding your own version of peace and paradise.' The sun-filled glasses tinkled.

This far from town, the beach was deserted. Mirri and Josef enjoyed the ocean and lying together on the warm sand at the edges of the rainforest.

'I'll go.' Josef was a blurry shadow in Mirri's sleepy vision.

'Go where?'

'We need wine and supplies, so I'll go. You stay here.'

'Mmm, if you insist.' Mirri rolled over and dozed.

In town, Josef loaded up with supplies and turned for home.

'Hey.'

Josef turned to see the old-mate from the newspaper shop post office combo waving a package at him.

'Are you still staying up at Mirri's?'

'I am.'

'This looks important. You wanna take it with you?' He handed Josef a priority paid parcel.

'Thanks.' Josef sat it on top of the box of supplies and headed up the track.

Mirri woke startled. Someone was on the beach and they sounded angry. She grabbed up her gear and turned to head for the path to home when she saw Josef. His was the angry voice. He was looking out to sea. He was ranting, sobbing. She ran towards him. Something must have happened in town.

'Josef, what's wrong?' She put her hand on his arm. He recoiled from her touch.

'Fuck off.' He walked away up the beach.

She chased him. Grabbed him. 'What's going on?'

'I saw it.'

'You saw what, Josef?'

'Your lab.'

Mirri was dizzy. 'What?' She was sure she'd heard wrong.

'The old-mate at the post office gave me a parcel for you.' He was breathing fast. 'The label on the parcel said keep in a cool dry place or some crap, so I thought I'd put it in your lab.'

'How?'

'It's not a big place, I guessed which key.'

'You shouldn't—'

'I fucking know now why you'd say I shouldn't.' Tears streamed down Josef's face. 'There was a journal on the counter near the door. I knocked it to the floor when I put the parcel down, and it fell open.'

'Shit.'

'Shit indeed,' he yelled. 'I read some stuff on the open pages. I didn't believe it, so I read more.' He shook his head. 'Then the cold room.' He was gagging. 'Please tell me I've got this all terribly wrong.'

Mirri stared. 'Josef, it's not the way you think.' She stepped up to touch him.

He pushed her back. 'Am I wrong that you have a cold room full of body parts and brains in jars?' His breath was a growl. 'Where did you get them? Shit. Where did the parts of me come from?' He shook his head 'Please tell me your father is really in that grave at the back of the garden.'

'Of course he is.'

'This has got to be some bizarre joke.' Tears flowed and he heaved a trembling breath. 'I'm going back to the life I understand. Away from this bullshit.' He ran down the beach towards town.

Mirri stood, swaying in the shock-wave of how horribly things had unfolded. She loved Josef. He was a kind and wonderful man and she had broken his heart. More than that, she had broken his life and his identity. She watched him run, but didn't follow him. She knew what would happen when he tried returning to his old life. A life that was real to him but conjured by her. She just hoped his connection to this place was strong enough.

All through that night and the next day, Mirri waited. To distract herself she scoured over her notes, reading over neural scripts, and revising formulas and telomere outputs. Josef did not deserve to be a victim to her bungling, like her father was. Lying on the daybed, exhausted, she stared up at the stars, ruminating about what to say to the local authorities. Running various ugly scenarios through her head.

Mirri woke to the sound of quiet crying. Josef sat huddled on the edge of the verandah. She stepped quietly over and touched his shoulder.

'None of it was real,' he whispered and sniffed. 'None of the people in my memories exist.'

'I'm so sorry about what happened.'

'I'm not real.'

'You're very real, Josef.'

'What did you do to me?' he hissed. 'To my head? To my heart? I have beautiful memories of being loved by my aunt. I loved my aunt and she only existed in my head. Because of you.' His breath hitched. 'And I should hate you. I should run and keep running, but I'm drawn to this place.'

She took his hands in hers. 'Remember that feeling,' she said, 'back in the first few days. That feeling of belonging here, at the house, with me.'

He nodded, shrugged, tears flowed.

'The reason you have those feelings is because they are true. Every motivation I had in my work was to lovingly create a person. When my father died, we were trying to use this science to save him. Because of love. We were working on this project so that others who were going to lose someone they love wouldn't have to. Our greatest hope was that the work we were doing would save people from that pain. Everything about your creation was about love, respect and kindness. You are a miracle and you belong here.'

'I want to hate you.' He stood and walked towards the gate.

'I don't expect you to forgive me any time soon,' she called after him, 'but I hope you'll learn to understand and know how amazing you are. Let me help you live your best life, whatever that is for you.'

The gate rattled on its hinges and he was gone.

At sunset, Josef walked up onto the verandah and poured wine into the glass she'd set on the table for him, out of habit. 'Did you make me love you?' he stared into the glass.

'What do you mean?'

'When you made me, did you make it so that I would love you.' He stared at her. 'Or are these feelings mine ... are they real?'

She spluttered, swallowed her wine and returned his gaze. 'I made a biography to be a base for your memories, planted neurological seeding to set up—'

'In English please.'

'I made a base storyline, but your brain is your brain and ditto for your heart. I didn't program you to have these new, current feelings.'

'Can I go if I want to?'

'You can go, anywhere you want, whenever you want.' Her heart squeezed. 'I'll help you with whatever you want to do.'

Hands clenched. Josef stood facing Mirri before taking a seat. He took her hand and placed the heart-stone in her palm. 'I want to stay here, with you.'

BUTTERFLY

gary david

I lay on my side, the cold stone floor beneath me amplifies the pain of the sword through my left breast and out my back. A dagger's tearing grip splits my inner thigh. The weight of the sword's unyielding intrusion tilts my face towards the stone, dictating my only possible posture.

With each faltering heartbeat my consciousness echoes off into haunting memories of my lost infant and her father. I see again those familiar eyes—cruelly extinguished from existence long ago. The warm sight of Midja, rolling in the mountain grass, in play with our cherished baby girl, Butterfly, dance like phantoms in my fading vision. A bitter-sweet ballet of what was, and will never be.

Death, a yearned-for path back to Butterfly, now looms as a daunting precipice. As the moment to let go nears, a tumultuous wave of doubt anchors me back, tethering me to this realm with invisible chains.

What if, beyond my final heartbeat, there lies only reverberating silence void of life? No one left to remember her, or the melody of her mischievous laugh. In this liminal space between life and death, I find myself grappling with an unexpected fear—not of dying, but of losing her memory forever in the finality of nothingness. This is a pain I find myself not ready to relinquish.

My father's voice, cold and unyielding, echoes with a chilling ultimatum to another in the room. 'If she dies, so do you.' His departure amplifies the outside celebration of my slayer—the Prince who, with a sword's brutal thrust through my chest plate, has claimed his right to marry me.

This savage ritual, a legacy of our ancestors, compels princes and princesses to prove the worthiness of their magic. The victor wins not only a spouse but the twin crowns of marriage and sovereignty. A duel that would kill anyone without healing magic. Someone like me.

The door slams, shutting out the ballroom crowd. My focus returns to the sword impaled in my chest. Blood trickles down the blade, dripping along the rain-guard before spattering to the growing pool on the floor.

I drift off again. A memory of my mother surfaces from before she died, her voice a soothing echo. She speaks of butterflies. 'After building their cocoon they endure immense trauma. With exception of a few core cells, their very being dissolves into vulnerable liquid. After this trauma, it either rebuilds into something more beautiful, or it slowly dies.'

As I watch each drop of blood jumping ship from my failing life, I lay, feeling akin to that dissolving caterpillar, not destined to emerge with new wings, but fading, failing to change into something more beautiful.

Abruptly, I ascend as though lifted by an invisible table. I find myself rolling onto my back. The sword in my chest, now pointing harmlessly downwards, easing the agony momentarily.

A light approaches, projecting my elongated shadow against the castle tapestries. A touch at my ankle startles me, jolting my eyes open into a blur of clotting blood.

'How long has your healing magic been dormant?' The voice is deep, but not familiar.

I try to speak but only manage to wheeze.

The stranger's hands gently surround the entry wound of the sword. The fragile torn flesh glows red through his fingers.

My consciousness drifts back to my daughter, the first time she caught a baby firefly. The fragile insect eager to escape like the light between Butterfly's tiny fingers. In that gentle moment, my heart swelled with warmth, witnessing the instinctive kindness with which she cradled the tiny life. Her delicate fingers forming a protective haven, a sanctuary of love for the fragile firefly.

'Your healing magic,' the insistent voice anchors me back. 'How long?'

My mind scrambles to get its bearings. I welcome a fresh, unclotted breath. 'A few years. Ever since ...' The words I have never spoken out loud refuse to escape.

With every blink the bloodshot tears dilute. The man's features crystallise into focus as a mysterious light, no larger than a fist, trails his shoulder. He is perhaps a decade my senior.

My eyes widen, my failing heart quickens at the sight of the spirit.

'Calm yourself, you are safe.'

'You're a Necron.'

'Yes.'

The curious light moves closer to my eyes. 'Get that thing away from me.'

The spirit startles back.

'Drawing magic from the dead is forbidden here.' My distress disturbs the sword buried deep in my chest, triggering a scream the warrior inside of me doesn't take pride in, I gasp and wait for the pain to reduce. 'Why would my father employ a Necron?'

'Is there nothing you would not do to keep your only daughter alive?'

His question lingers in the air, heavy with implications. I'm lost in the shame of not keeping Butterfly alive. If given the opportunity, would I plunder magic from the dead preventing them from crossing over and finding peaceful passage. I fear what I would become if my despair was given that choice.

'Trapping innocent souls is barbaric beyond any measurement,' I answer.

'More barbaric than princes slaying princesses to determine whose magic is worthy of marriage?'

'These realms have been destroying each other for centuries. The kingdom will fall if the magical bloodlines give birth to weaker heirs.'

'It's your family's addiction to power and conflict that endangers the kingdom, Princess. Not bloodlines.'

Although this is an argument I have made to my family many times, I still feel the need to defend them. 'It's more complicated than that.'

'People only choose complexity when they lack courage.'

His assessment of my courage stings. My attention moves uneasily to the approaching light. 'I don't want the dead inside me.'

'You find the steel inside you more appealing?'

I glare at his sarcasm, but have no choice but to abandon my argument. 'What was that … before it died?'

'She was barely a few years old. I am trying to help her crossover, but she resists. You would like her. She's every bit as stubborn as you.'

'She?' My memories fight to escape through my tears. I distract myself. 'If she crosses over, won't you lose your magic?'

'I will lose her magic, not mine. She's a powerful healer. I will miss that very much.' His voice wavers. 'But I will miss her more.'

My breath slows and my tension reduces. 'Why help her?'

'I don't know.' He breathes, deep in thought. 'Maybe because it would hurt more not to.'

I was raised on the nightmarish stories of Necrons killing innocents to harvest their magic. Yet, the man before me seems an ill fit for such malevolent narratives. Overwhelmed by my confusion, I find myself compelled to ask, 'Why did you become a ... Necron?'

'When sleep took me one night, I had no idea I would awaken to an arrow puncturing my chest. For days, teetering on the brink of death, my body grew colder until the afterlife's light called. She screamed "no" and wouldn't let me follow it. After she healed me, becoming a Necron wizard was the only way to help her.'

'You only use her magic to heal?'

'It's the only magic she will let me use. If I go to a dark place, she traps me in an incantation mist till I return to peace. I was stuck in the first one for weeks.' He smiles. 'She's very loving. Let her show you.'

He cradles my leg with the softest of touches. His fingers trace a path upwards to the broken off dagger in my upper thigh. His hands glow as soft as his touch. I breathe in a human connection I have not felt in a long time.

'Are you okay, Princess?'

'Princesses are a protected species in my world. We are rarely handled by strange men.'

'Okay, we will take this slow.'

That's the worst thing he could do right now. I close my eyes and my mind follows his hands, pulling my thigh to his hips, supporting the wound. I have underestimated how my body has missed this type of touch.

The glow above his shoulder drops into his collar bone, through his arm, out his palm and into my thigh. I cry out, unready for his magic to rip the dagger from my leg into his hands. The light shoots from within the wound, closing it almost instantly.

'Let's take a look at this sword, shall we?'

However the glow has other ideas. I feel it move from the closing wound to my womb. It stops.

'What's she doing?' My heart races.

'Come on little one. Keep it moving.' He directs.

I feel like I am betraying my ... 'Get her out of there,' I cry.

I breathe easier as she abandons my womb and moves towards the sword instead.

The light touches the blade and is then shot out the weapon. With a scream, she crashes into the ceiling. Undeterred, she flies straight back through the sword. Only to be evicted twice as hard with another crash to the ceiling.

The wizard holds his hand out and faces it up. The light complies and heads to his palm.

'She is becoming powerful, but still has much to learn.'

'I have never seen a magic sword like this,' I reply.

'This sword has no magic.'

I pause. My head tilts.

'Just as emotion can create magic, so too can it block it.'

His words fill me with more unrest than the sword protruding from my chest.

'Shall we talk about what you won't? Shall we speak about the child that once lived in this womb?'

'I can't.'

'Even if it means death?'

His words irritate me. I grip the handle tight with both hands and push out the blade from my chest, but the sword thrusts back in all the way. The handle, now pushing into my chest, pinning me down hard to the invisible table.

'Stop it!' I scream in agony.

He steps forward just out of reach. 'Tell me about the child!'

'No.'

'What was her name?' he yells.

I look away.

'Her name?' he yells louder.

'Bapala.' I scream back. My head collapses in tears.

The intensity of his voice retreats.

'Her father was indigenous to these lands. My name sounds like the word cocoon in his language.' I breathe, I cry. 'Bapala means butterfly to his people.'

'Why was she killed?'

'What?'

'Why!' he raises his voice, closing the gap, eyes wide open as if I were prey.

The light flies between us and yells, 'No.'

He steps away, but a mist of magic cocoons the Necron. He punches the mist in anger, impacting it as if a stone wall.

'What's going on?' I demand.

He screams in frustration, takes a breath and falls to a seated defeat.

'Help me take the sword out,' I plea.

'I can't. There's no way to walk through the mist until all my anger is gone, and love and peace returns. She can't control it. She's protective of you.'

He looks to the floor. A grief I am familiar with.

'Is she your child?'

He remains silent. I know that look. Trapped in memories that will torture you if you dare speak their secrets.

'It was my job to protect her. I failed,' he says.

His words help me find a small amount of courage. 'When I came of age, it became very real to me I would have to marry to strengthen the magical bloodlines. They were trying to marry me off in the middle of a defiant stage.' My voice trembles in uncharted territory. I try to speak what I have never spoken before. 'I fell in love with a local indigenous boy called Midja. We both wanted to escape our destiny. He was the only one who could make me laugh in the years drowned in family bickering. If our love persisted our worlds would tear themselves apart. We feared we would only hasten to war, the realms we longed to harmonise. Ultimately, we acknowledged reality and embraced our responsibilities.' My hand snakes around to rest on my abdomen as a tear escapes. 'That was, until Bapala. When our parents found out about the baby, they were infuriated we had contaminated thousands of years of magical bloodlines. They called to end the pregnancy. So ... we ran away.'

I contemplate, with deep regret, all the damage done by two teenagers falling in love. 'After I gave birth, wizards from my kingdom tracked us down. I thought they would take us back to the castle, so I didn't resist. But they ...' Tears well up. '...

killed Midja and Butterfly.' My voice croaks, finding it difficult to speak. 'A relentless torment of grief, shame, and regret erodes my mind every day. My Mother would always speak of transforming trauma into something more beautiful, but I failed at that too.

'I'm afraid that to heal, to move on, I have to let go of this pain. But painful memories are all I have left of them.'

The light drifts towards the sword, morphing into the image of a young child, barely older than a toddler looking down at me. Her smile is a bittersweet reminder of my long-gone baby, unleashing a torrent of tears. When I look at her, I miss Butterfly.

She floats upwards as the sword follows, exiting my chest.

Magic fills me like an old friend and protector, healing every cut and scrape that litters my body. I sit up without pain. I look at the Necron on the other side of the mist. The child floats between us. I smile. 'Thank you,' I say with a loving sincerity I've not felt in years.

'I must go. The marriage ceremony awaits, along with my future husband.' I cringe, speaking such a word as husband in the Necron's presence. 'Will you attend? The kingdom owes you a debt.'

He remains silent.

'The magic bonding ceremony is a beautiful sight if you have not seen one before.'

'I can't pass through the mist without peace or love,' he says, 'I cannot be at peace with this marriage. The kingdom needs you to lead. Not your fiancé.'

'He's the strongest wizard in the kingdom. He will keep us all safe from our enemies.'

'With you leading, there will be no enemies.'

I step to the edge of the mist and place my hand against it. I feel nothing. Stepping through it, I grasp his hands and bend my forehead to touch his. Deep within my soul, I hope he would let me kiss him. He does not move his lips to mine. Out of duty I can't move mine to his. He looks up for a brief moment, my heart jumps, but he looks away. I must leave him before my weakness endangers the kingdom once more.

My weakness almost finds the courage to kiss him, when the child separates our foreheads.

I smile. 'I hope the two of you find peace one day.' I raise my head and examine his sad eyes. I look at the child, hoping it's not the last time. I step back. He steps forward, but the mist won't let him follow.

I turn and place my hand on the door handle, not sure if I want to walk through it and to the future that awaits me. I look back to see if he has the courage of speech I lack. I breathe deep once. I breathe deep again. I open the door and step through into the arms of a thankful father, and a cheering crowd.

'We are gathered here today to join these two kingdoms, these two people, these two hearts.'

The priest is dressed in iridescent golden robes, like the wise elders of our past. My fiancé is outfitted in newer ceremonial attire. More handsome than any dream I had as a child. All the important members of the kingdom are present, dressed in their most expensive wardrobes. Everything exceeds my fantasies. The most handsome, powerful prince in all the lands is mine. My

39

magic has returned to full strength. This is everything I have ever dreamed of.

And yet without Butterfly, without Midja, I don't feel any of it.

A tear falls. I turn to my father, who mistakes my tears for happiness, and he smiles with joy in return. I remind myself, the safety of the kingdom is more important than my happiness.

'Prince of the East, do you give freely your magic in service of the kingdoms? In service of the family? In service of your princess?'

'I do.' An enchanting glow originates deep within his chest, steadily amplifying in brightness as it rises into the vast expanse of the grand old cathedral.

'Princess of the West, do you give freely your magic in service of the kingdoms? In service of the family? In service of your prince?'

'I do.' The same magic glows in me and rises next to his.

'Without further ado, what war has splintered over thousands of years, let marriage bring back together. Let the magical bloodlines from these two ancient families join for now and until the end of our time.'

The entire room watches our magical glows move towards each other. Anticipation of the merge into a stronger, more powerful magic, silences the room.

A silence that is shattered by the piercing shriek of a child, 'No!' A spirit outline of a child races up to separate our magic glows.

My father shouts before unleashing a magical projectile into the air. A twirling beam of coloured light with a treacherous sting at the end of its rainbow, collides with the child, pinning her against the ceiling. Magic streams from other families are directed to the battlefront above. The child struggles to escape as explosion after explosion pins her back.

The Necron wizard appears from the back of the room, 'Stop! She's only a child, she doesn't understand.'

My father's intolerance sends a stream, knocking the wizard to the floor. 'Reveal,' he cries.

The wizard de-ages ten years as his skin darkens.

'Midja,' I whisper to myself. I look up. 'Butterfly,' I cry.

'You,' my father rages.

My father and Midja engage, each striving to land their magic blows. I am powerless. My magic is high in the air now vulnerable for anyone to destroy.

'Stop the ritual,' I call.

My father hisses to the priest, 'Finish it.'

The priest starts to chant. Our magic draws closer when Butterfly sends a stream to my magic and surrounds it in mist. My fiancé's magic is unable to penetrate it to finish the bonding ritual.

'His magic has no love,' I murmur.

Midja sprays a light of magic towards the priest, and it's blocked by my father. Without Bapala's magic, Midja crouches down, trying to shield himself from my father's deadly intent.

'Stop!' Unable to watch this unfold for a second time, I charge the priest, knocking him to the ground. My striking fists keep his mouth from chanting. I jump off to dodge a light stream. I use the priest as a shield to block another. He drops unconscious to the floor. My magic hurries back to me. But so does my fiancé's. He joins the fight against Midja. The barrage of magic streams overwhelm my ability to defend them both. I send from my palms light flashes to distract my father. Another to defend Midja. Another to defend Butterfly.

Midja starts to rise, and becomes more powerful. Somehow, he's tapping into Butterfly. He overcomes my father. Light streams are flashing and colliding everywhere.

'His magic comes from the dead,' my father cries. 'Destroy the spirit.' All the guests' streams direct to Butterfly.

'Bapala, no,' Midja cries.

An almighty bang thunders through the hall. Rebounding light throws everyone back, and me to the floor, stopping all streams in their tracks. Butterfly falls in front of me with a thud, hitting the floor as if her light has a solid mass. Injured, she crawls toward me as I sit up.

Blasts continue at Butterfly. Numerous beams strike her and ricochet perilously past me, as she screams in a pitch I cannot bear to hear.

Midja charges in front of Butterfly to shield us both.

Injured, Butterfly continues her limped crawl.

Blood flows from Midja's chest, arms, and legs. He struggles to stay upright but refuses to move out of the path of Butterfly.

My fiancé steps forward, 'Move, Necron,'

Midja replies with a defiant gaze.

My fiancé fires magic into Midja. It splits into two, past his defending palm and hits him on both shoulders. Midja hits the ground but stands again in defiance.

Bapala crawls closer. Midja looks back to her, then forward. The Prince splits another beam, and Midja catches them in both palms before throwing them back to overwhelm my fiancé. As the beam pushes forward against the Prince's defence, his destruction seems certain, until my father's beam hits Midja from the side. He can no longer lift his arms. He's defenceless. Two more streams to his chest and he crashes to the ground.

My child crawls up my leg and on top of my stomach. She looks up at me trembling, but I don't know how to help. She passes through my skin, finding refuge in my womb. I place my hands over her, and tears fall.

Motherhood fills my heart once more, and my magic glows strong. It moves towards the child's fragile spirit and creates a protective cocoon around her. I feel her pain ebbing away, healing in the sanctity of my womb.

An old memory activates. My mother's voice, 'Grow,' she says, 'into something more beautiful.'

I look down to Bapala, our two magics merge and my heartbeat speeds up. The veins leading to my palms feel electrified. The magic builds, wanting to release. The fearful pant of my breath slows, and becomes relaxed and deep. Everyone seems to slow down. I close my eyes.

'The Princess is a Necron,' a voice cries. 'Kill her.'

Hundreds of beams fly towards Midja to get to me.

Midja lifts his head, his eyes shutting in resignation as he braces himself for death.

I raise my hand and surround him with mist.

His face turns from a tight clench to surprise. He looks back at me.

I walk through the mist. Tears fall, only this time in joy, and in love.

He places his palms on my cheeks and kisses me like he did when we were young. His kiss transitions to a tight, protective hug. My tears release years of grief.

Bapala wiggles between us, and we laugh. Her mischievous giggle completes our family once again.

The mist's edge pounded by hundreds of beams, conceals the outside world in a spectrum of rainbow light.

'I told you the bonding ceremony was beautiful.' We hug and I can't help but cry again when Bapala rests her head against mine. 'Hello, beautiful girl,' I say as a mother. Something I never thought I would get to do again.

One by one, the beams exhaust, until they all stop. The entire ballroom stands in silence, watching us embrace.

'Stay here.' I walk through the mist to address the two families.

My fiancé steps forward and yells, 'How dare you?' The streams of magic fly again and I raise my palm. The streams disappear before they find their target. As the smoke dissipates, all the attackers are now ensnared in mist. They slowly comprehend the reality of their prison.

I look differently at the people I once considered friends.

44

'Many of you will die in these magical cages. For those of you who learn to overcome your anger, and love again, you will be free to help me lead this world into a new age.'

My father pushes against the mist. 'What have you done?'

'You killed my child.' Sadness stirs within me as I feel the answer he dares not speak. 'We can no longer kill for peace.'

'Don't be naïve,' he spits. 'You will give our enemies the opportunity to destroy us all.'

'If we can't learn to lead with love, it's not us who should be allowed to lead.'

I return to Midja as if we are the only ones in the room. Bapala rubs her forehead to mine.

'You have found your mother again, little one, are you ready to cross over now?' He smiles.

'No!' she defies and flies back into my womb. Midja and I grin. I embrace him. 'What do we do now?' he asks.

'I guess we take our lives, our people and our lands and we do what we should have always done.' I place my hand over my womb. 'Just like a butterfly, we emerge into something more beautiful.'

BRUCE

robin martin thomas

Butterflies rioted in her stomach as Maddie used her upgraded security pass to enter the hallowed atmosphere of Lab 3 of Real Tech. Casey, chief supervisor on this project, burst through a door, lab coat flapping behind him.

'Maddie? Geoff said you were on the way. Follow me.' He swiped his ID on a steel-plated door, guiding her to a small room.

Stepping inside, Maddie stopped.

Every female's fantasy stood next to the computers. Her pulse quickened, and her breath caught. Chestnut hair drifted over his forehead and the chiseled chin had a dimple. A black T-shirt stretched over a broad chest, and designer jeans moulded his long legs. Intense brown eyes looked into hers.

Or so it seemed. She looked again—but they didn't blink.

Casey turned to her. 'What do you think?'

She exhaled a deep breath, as realisation and disappointment hit her in equal measure. 'Is this ...? I can't believe it. He looks so real.'

'He should be—we've been working on him for at least five years. Bruce is even more impressive in action.'

Stepping closer, Maddie reached out to touch the face. Instead of the synthetic smoothness she expected, his 'skin' was soft like the real thing. She brushed her hand over his silky hair. This wasn't a cheap wig they'd attached at the top. Even his smell was human, with the slight scent of Armani. They'd worked out every detail.

'You'd almost think he was human.'

'And he almost is. He's the first android using Generative Artificial Intelligence.' Casey went over to a computer in the corner. 'I'm about to start activation. Once I do, Bruce will remain 'live' for about fifteen days, so you shouldn't have to do anything. If you need any help, my number is included in the information emailed to you.'

'Can you just run through everything again?'

'Haven't you read your task outline?'

'Geoffrey only sent it this morning when he told me I was selected for this job. Of course, it's a tremendous honour—'

'That's right, you weren't the first choice.'

Her lips tightened. She might have known. She was aware of her insignificant status, something she was hoping to change.

Casey continued, 'The other two had to drop out because of other commitments. Geoff said you'd be up to it.' He raised an eyebrow.

'Yes, definitely.'

'Basically, you'll expose Bruce to as many different situations as possible over the next two weeks. Real Tech wants to launch him for commercial use. This is one of the final tests to ensure he's ready as the "all-purpose android". Keep a log of your activities and how Bruce performs in each task. When you go to sleep, simply tell him to deactivate. When you're ready to use him again, just say, "activate". Read the information sent, but really, that's it.'

'Can you tell me about Bruce?' In her job as an assistant researcher, she'd been exposed to very little information about this cutting-edge AI droid.

'Bruce is a collaborative effort. But the brainchild behind this creation is Andrew Long. He's a genius. He'll be reading your report with great interest.' Casey looked at his watch. 'I've a meeting shortly, so let's get started.'

He bent over his computer again, and within seconds there was a whirring sound and a click. 'Activate.'

Bruce moved his head and looked at them.

'Good afternoon. Casey.' His voice was deep, melodious, natural.

'I do not believe we have met before.' His eyes turned in her direction.

'This is Maddie. You're going to be staying with her for a while. She'll help you get used to different social situations and interactions.'

Bruce extended his hand. 'Hello, Maddie. It is a pleasure to meet you.'

His hand, warm and firm, closed around hers.

'Hi Bruce.' She shivered. He seemed so real.

Bruce turned to face Casey. 'Will you be helping with my socialisation too, Casey?'

'I'm not part of Maddie's social circle. But we've vetted her family and friends. We're confident you'll be safe. I'll be on call if necessary.'

Maddie felt the heat rise to her face. 'You investigated my family and friends? Without my permission!'

'You gave your permission in the employment agreement you signed two years ago. You hardly think we'd let an investment worth millions of dollars go out the door without ensuring its security first.'

She'd signed so many forms when she started work at Real Tech it was hard to remember what they all were. 'I don't like the privacy of my friends and family being invaded—without them even knowing.'

Casey sighed, putting his hands on his hips. 'We were discreet and took every precaution. You're not just taking a microwave oven home. I thought Geoff prepared you for this. If you don't want the job, speak up now.'

He had a point. If she didn't take this opportunity Maddie feared she'd never be offered another one again.

'I'll do it.'

'I believe you have upset Maddie. Her temperature is elevated, her heart rate has increased, and her skin is flushed,' Bruce said.

Maddie lifted her eyebrows. 'You can tell all that?'

Bruce nodded. 'Yes, I have been programmed with highly perceptive senses. Even now, Casey is downloading information about you into my program.'

She looked over at Casey, who was still at the computer.

'This will make it easier for Bruce to assist you and anticipate your needs. Every Bruce that eventually makes it to market will be programmed with information about its owner.'

'My mission is to serve you, Maddie.'

She could get on board with that.

Casey straightened and turned to face her. 'You're good to go.'

'I take him in my car back to my apartment, just like that?'

Casey nodded. 'We want to make Bruce simple enough for anyone to operate. I'll walk you out. Bruce, follow us.'

Once they reached the carpark, she led the way to her small Suzuki.

'Any trouble, contact me.' Casey assisted Bruce into the car and closed the door. 'And don't mess this up. This droid is worth millions.'

Starting the engine, Maddie muttered, 'Casey is such an asshole.'

'At least he did not compare you to a microwave oven,' Bruce said.

Maddie laughed. 'Bruce, you just made a joke.'

'Yes, my creator added a sense of humour to my program. I have twenty-eight personality attributes. It makes me the most versatile and advanced android in the world.'

'Is modesty one of your attributes?'

'No, that is not part of my program.'

Obviously understanding sarcasm wasn't either, she thought.

When she unlocked the door to her small unit, Maddie sighed. Her dressing gown was draped over the couch, Ugg boots were scattered on the floor, and her coffee cup was on the table. She didn't even want to think about the dishes in the kitchen sink or her unmade bed. She'd been in a rush this morning. She was only human. Thankfully, Bruce was not.

Bruce looked around. 'I will tidy up. I'm programmed to help.'

She started to say something, then stopped. He was right. That's why he was here—to test his programming.

It was weird, seeing this man-like robot move around her apartment, picking things up. It reminded her of Ned, her ex, who'd moved out six months ago. Not that she missed him. God, no.

Over the next few days, Maddie started to get used to Bruce. He helped with laundry and housework, and even watched TV with her in the evening.

There were a few mishaps, like the morning he made her coffee with salt rather than sugar. Or when he put her socks in the dishwasher instead of the washing machine. But, for the most part, he was doing well.

She decided it was time for the next step. 'Maybe tomorrow, we'll go out for coffee.'

Bruce's face lit up like a child promised a toy. She felt a surge of affection that such a small treat brought him so much pleasure.

The next day, they went to Frank's, the local café. Maddie was amused to see the girls at the next table check him out. What would they think if they knew he was a robot?

Bruce, oblivious, looked at Maddie. I will try small talk, which will enable me to socialise. You look pretty today, Maddie.'

'You scrub up well too.'

'Pardon? I never need to wash.'

She smiled. 'Don't say that—unless you want people to avoid you. Scrub up well means you look okay, handsome even.'

His smile widened. 'Maddie is a nice name. Is it a nickname?'

'Yes, my name is Madrid. My parents named me after the city they met each other. I shortened it to Maddie.'

Bruce nodded.

I'm actually making small talk with a robot, she thought. *And he's not bad at it.*

'I see,' he said, tilting his head. 'You are fortunate they didn't meet in Dildo.'

She spat her coffee out, splattering the table and his T-shirt. 'Bruce, you can't say that! It's totally inappropriate.'

He looked puzzled. 'I was making a joke. And there is an actual place named Dildo. It is a small fishing village in Canada. Did you not think it was funny?'

She tried not to smile. 'I think it's time we went home.'

As the week passed, Maddie decided to try a more challenging social encounter—a party.

When she told him, Bruce's eyes widened. 'Have you told your friends about me?'

Maddie hesitated. She was going to tell Betts, the party's host, about the droid, until she discovered her ex, Ned, would be there. So, she kept quiet. A mistake, probably. If Ned knew she was bringing a robot, he would think she was a total loser and couldn't get anyone else. She wouldn't give him that satisfaction.

Could Bruce pull it off and convince people he was real? It would be the ultimate test.

It was just for one night after all.

'Bruce, sit down.'

Sitting next to him, she said, 'Tonight will be a real test of your abilities.'

'Excellent. I welcome a challenge.'

'I haven't told my friends about you. They'll think you're human.'

He smiled. 'That will give me an opportunity to practise my social skills.'

'Can you make people think you are … human?'

She could hear the whirring of mechanisms inside him. Not a good sign.

'I believe with an 87.36 per cent chance I can.'

'Bruce, you can't talk like that. You must make your speech sound normal.'

'What do you mean?'

'Listen to the way people talk. Try to copy that.'

He nodded.

'One more important piece of information you should know. My ex will be there.'

'Your ex what?'

'My ex-boyfriend. We broke up six months ago. If he knows I'm bringing a robot to the party, he'll laugh at me.'

'Why?'

'He'll think I can't get a real boyfriend.'

'You want me to be your boyfriend?' His forehead wrinkled.

'I want you to pretend you're a human guy I'm bringing to the party. Can you do that?'

'Yes, Maddie. I'm already attracted to you.'

'Pardon?' This was getting beyond weird.

'It is programmed into me. We are meant to bond with our owners, like a dog to its master. It makes it easier for us to be the perfect servant.'

'Oh, I see.' Relief, but also disappointment, flooded her. Why? He was just a robot, wasn't he?

'So, what does a boyfriend do?'

'Stay close to me, say as little as possible.'

He nodded.

She crossed her fingers.

The music was booming when they arrived. Maddie took a deep breath. Bruce looked, even felt, human. It was how he was going to behave that worried her.

'Maddieeeeee!' Betts screamed as she opened the door and gave her a hug. 'You look fabulous!' She looked over at Bruce and one eyebrow lifted. 'And this is ...'

'Bruce.'

He held out his hand. 'Pleased to meet you. I am Maddie's boyfriend.'

Betts looked at Maddie with a surprised smile. 'Come on in, Bruce, and meet the gang.'

They moved to the lounge where her friends were seated.

'Hi guys,' she said.

'Hey, Maddie, glad you could make it,' Joel, Betts's partner, greeted her.

'I am Bruce, pleased to meet you. I am Maddie's boyfriend.'

Maddie gave a tight smile as she sensed everyone's heightened interest.

Joel gave Maddie an amused glance. 'Hey, man, make yourself at home. There's beer and wine outside on the patio.'

'Thanks, *man*.'

Before Bruce could say anything else, Maddie grabbed his hand and pulled him outside.

'Don't keep telling everyone you're my boyfriend,' she hissed.

'Who am I supposed to be?' His brow wrinkled in a now familiar way.

'A friend.'

She poured a glass of wine. Had she made a mistake bringing the droid here?

'Hey, Maddie,' said a familiar voice behind her.

Ned, long, blond hair pulled back in a ponytail, sat back with a vape in hand. *How much had he heard of her conversation with Bruce?*

'Ned,' She acknowledged him with a cool nod.

'You're looking good.'

'Where's Heidi?' She couldn't help ask about the woman he'd left her for.

'We decided to go our separate ways a while back.'

Wise woman, she thought. Heidi had worked out sooner than Maddie that Ned was not boyfriend material.

The droid moved forward. 'Hi, I am Bruce. I am not Maddie's boyfriend. I am her friend.'

Ned chuckled. 'Good to know, dude. Maddie and I go way back, don't we, darl?'

How did Ned manage to annoy her within the first thirty seconds of their meeting?

'Ancient history, Ned.' She forced a laugh. 'We've both moved on.'

Ned came closer. 'Maybe we could do a U-turn. I've been meaning to call you. When Betts said you'd be here tonight, I thought it'd be a good chance to, you know, re-connect.' He ran a hand down her arm, then looked at Bruce. 'Hey, dude, why don't you head inside and give Maddie and I a little space? We've got some catching up to do.'

Maddie stepped back. 'No, thanks, Ned. I don't make the same mistake twice.'

Bruce moved forward. 'Hey, *dude*, you are upsetting *darl*. Her temperature has risen by 0.95 degrees and her blood pressure is elevated. You should leave now.'

'Who the hell are you to tell me what to do?'

'Who the hell am I? I am Maddie's friend and I do not like anyone upsetting her.'

'Really? And what are you going to do about it?'

'I will show you.' Before she could stop him, Bruce put his hands on Ned's shoulders and lifted him up as if he were a rag doll.

'Bruce, stop!'

Bruce carried the kicking and swearing Ned through the house, opened the front door, and de-posited him on the front step. Closing the door, Bruce came back inside. Maddie's friends stared, open mouthed.

"Betts, I'm so sorry,' Maddie moaned.

Betts laughed. 'I wouldn't have missed that for the world.'

'Too right. He's an arse,' Joel said.

'We should go.' Maddie grabbed Bruce's hand.

Maddie couldn't get out of there quickly enough.

As they drove home, Maddie said, 'Bruce, how could you? That was a terrible thing to do.'

'I did not hurt him, Maddie.'

'You can't manhandle people just because they annoy you. I told you to stop and you ignored me.'

'My system overrode that for your protection.'

'He wasn't going to hurt me. He was just being a jerk.' Maddie pulled into her parking space. Getting out, she slammed the car door and walked to her unit. Bruce trailed behind her.

'I am sorry, Maddie. I do not believe I integrated properly into that social situation.'

'You totally failed, and you don't look one bit sorry.'

'Putting Ned outside was a satisfying action. Perhaps I should have said I was your boyfriend. That would have been satisfying too.' The crinkling of his eyes showed his amusement.

'Bruce, you're a robot.'

'True. But, in many ways I am superior to a human being. I would certainly make a better boyfriend than Ned. Maddie, I would like to try another human experience and go on a date—with you.'

She ignored the tightening of her stomach, and flutter of her pulse. Her tone was firm. 'No, Bruce. Not possible. Your purpose is to serve humans.'

'But if I learn more about humans then I will be able to serve them better. Dating is a social activity. I think I should try it.'

She didn't know whether to laugh or cry.

'Bruce, you're a droid. I'm a human being. Dating is a romantic relationship between two humans. I could no more date a robot than I could date ...' she thought for a moment, '... a microwave oven.' She knew she was being harsh, but she had to quash the feelings—in them both.

'That is not funny, Maddie.' Bruce's head slumped. 'I am a highly evolved creation with an intelligence greater than any human. I am stronger than humans. I even have emotions. In time, androids will be integrated into society. Not only will they perform jobs for humans, but they will also do them better. I am only the beginning of a new race of creations that one day will stand on equal footing with human beings.'

Maddie felt a wave of foreboding as she realised the truth of these words. Bruce was a machine, but a highly complex and advanced one. Would the line blur between humans and machines?

'I'm sorry, but that doesn't change my answer. People who date are attracted to each other. It's a human thing.'

'Don't you like me, Maddie. I like you.' His tone was wistful.

'You've been programmed to like me, but you're confusing that emotion with the attraction that two people feel for each other in a relationship.'

'You do not like me in the way you used to like Ned?'

'No, I'm sorry, Bruce.'

He was silent, then said, 'I need to deactivate now. My system is overloading.'

'Deactivate, Bruce.'

The night was long and restless. Maddie wrestled with her thoughts as she wrestled with her sheets. Bruce seemed so real that sometimes she forgot he wasn't. He was becoming too attached to her, and more worrying, she was beginning to have feelings too. Her pulse quickened when she saw him every morning, or when he gave her one of his megawatt smiles. She laughed at his jokes, felt his disappointment when he made a mistake, or his happiness when he succeeded at a task. He had a personality, quirky and sweet. It was part of his program. But was it much different from the genetic attributes people were born with?

In the morning, Maddie made one of the most difficult decisions of her life. Bruce was becoming so real to her that she almost wondered what it would be like to date him, even kiss him. And with that thought she knew—she had to return Bruce to Real Tech.

She called Casey.

Within the hour, he arrived. 'So, you weren't up to the job? Can't say I'm surprised.'

Bruce had more empathy than Casey.

'It's more complicated than that. Bruce started to have feelings for me. And he didn't always follow my instructions.'

'Impossible. He's a robot. He's programmed to know your needs. You've misinterpreted that as emotion. If he didn't follow your instructions, you weren't specific enough. We shouldn't have given you this task. You're obviously unqualified for the job.'

'You'll find ample evidence in my report to support what I'm saying.'

'There's no point in discussing this anymore. Email your report tomorrow when you return to work.'

There was so much she wanted to say, but looking at Casey's face, Maddie realised it was pointless. 'Will Andrew Long, his creator, want to contact me?'

Perhaps he'd be more receptive to what she had to say.

'I doubt it.' Casey turned to Bruce. 'Activate.'

'Good morning, Maddie. Casey, you have come for a visit.'

'We're returning to the lab, Bruce. The experiment is at an end. Follow me to the car.'

Bruce's eyes widened. 'I do not understand. I was making good progress. You do not wish me to go, do you Maddie?'

'I'm sorry, Bruce, but it's best.' Tears filled her eyes.

'But we like each other.'

'Good-bye, Bruce. You've done well, but it's time to go.'

'I do not want to go. I will not comply.' Bruce frowned and folded his arms.

'Move,' Casey shouted.

'No.'

'Deactivate,' Casey barked.

Bruce went motionless.

Casey scowled at Maddie. 'What the hell have you done to his programming? You may have jeopardised millions of dollars of research. I just hope we can fix it.'

'I've done nothing, I told you. Perhaps there's more to AI then you realise. Maybe, one day, androids will evolve to take their place alongside humans. Before that happens, you'd better get it right. And that, Casey, is on people like you, not me.'

As Casey drove away, Maddie let the tears fall. Knowing Bruce had been an incredible experience and she would never regret the opportunity she'd had, even if it meant losing her job. As she went upstairs, she realised she'd miss Bruce far more than she ever did Ned.

A week later, she got a phone call from an unknown number.

'Maddie?'

It sounded like Bruce.

'Yes.' Her voice was shaky.

'Andy Long here. I'm Bruce's creator. I'd like to talk to you about your recent experiences with him. Are you free for lunch?'

In shock, she answered, 'Yes, of course.'

'Great. Let's meet around noon at Frank's. I believe you took Bruce there once. See you then.'

61

Bruce's creator didn't sound unfriendly, but it didn't stop her worrying. Had she somehow ruined the droid?

At noon, she swung through the door at Frank's—and stopped.

His dark hair fell over his forehead in a familiar way.

'Bruce?'

He smiled and her heart quickened.

'Hi Maddie, pleasure to meet you. I'm Andy.'

Her heart sank, but she smiled as she shook his hand.

'Have a seat.'

She sank into a chair. 'You look and sound just like him.'

'That's because I programmed him to be like me. I even gave him my middle name.'

'For a moment, I thought ...'

'I was him? Then I did my job. You formed a bond with Bruce, didn't you?'

She nodded. 'As he did with me, although Casey disagrees.'

Andy shrugged. 'Casey is an excellent technician, but he doesn't always appreciate the full spectrum of possibilities with AI creations. You do, which is why I wanted to talk to you. I'm excited about Bruce's evolving program and his capabilities for both advanced emotional responses and autonomy. But I'm also aware of the need for caution.'

'Then you believe me?'

'I found the comments in your report both interesting and insightful.'

As they talked over lunch, Maddie found they had a natural rapport.

'I see why Bruce liked you, Maddie,' Andy said.

She felt the warmth flood her cheeks. She started to see why she had liked Bruce. He had been the introduction to the real thing. When Andy smiled, her pulse quickened. When his eyes caught hers, her breath stopped. It was confusing, but also exciting. She wanted to explore these feelings more.

'I think we're going to need more meetings to discover that bond between you and Bruce,' Andy said, leaning towards her.

'There's certainly a lot to talk about.' She looked down at the table where their hands were almost touching.

'Maddie, nice name, is it short for anything?'

She was about to tell him, then she hesitated.

'Just Maddie,' she said and smiled. Time enough to discover whether Bruce's creator had the same sense of humour.

And this time, if Andy were to ask her for a date, she knew exactly what her answer would be.

THE GUEST ROOM

sarah hegerty

I should say something.

I'm sitting in the lobby of the virtual reality app *The Guest Room*, waiting for Casper to login. We've been talking for weeks now and my free trial is about to run out. I still haven't mentioned the accident — or the consequences of it.

Casper's name appears in my user list and our private Guest Room loads.

Our avatars load into the Basic Guest Room Environment, seated opposite each other on grey sofas. The walls are pale grey. The ceiling and floors are matte white. Between us is a generic boxy white coffee table anchoring a charcoal shag to the floor. The outside environment doesn't even render. Like you're supposed to pay extra for happiness. I remind myself I'm here for the company.

I want to tell Casper the truth—and still be accepted. But I'm terrified. Before the accident I was an adventure loving nut, just like them. It's why they're so easy to talk to. Our spirits are kindred. But now—for me—the experiences are just memories.

'Hey you.' Casper's gentle voice.

'Hey.'

'Your trial period ends next week, doesn't it?'

The question slams into me like a sledgehammer. Obliterates my fantasy. I fumble one of the VR controllers in the moment of disorientation. It smashes against the tiles. I wince holding my breath. 'Yeah. So, why waste time?'

'I don't want it to end next week.'

Me either, but there's no way to answer this without telling them the truth. I half slip my headset up so I can see where my controller landed and realise it's fallen out of reach. I rest my other controller in my lap and wheel my chair carefully forward coming to a stop beside the controller so I can reach down and reclaim it. Awkwardly, using my chair as a counterbalance with my other arm, while my legs remain useless dead weight in the chair. As one hand wraps around the controller a wheel starts to lift but I manage to recentre my weight before tipping all the way over. I relax back into the chair with a heavy sigh. I'm still getting used to this.

'Did I say something wrong?'

Oh, crap. I didn't reply. 'No. It's not that.'

'Why do you sound so relieved then?'

'It's just I dropped my controller awkwardly and had to pick it up. I was distracted. Sorry.' The truth, at least.

'Oh. You seem a little evasive. *Do* you want it to end next week?'

'Of course not.' But I think it will. 'I've told you things are ... difficult for me right now. I can't afford a subscription, maybe down the track though.'

Casper's avatar is statue still and quiet for so long I'm convinced they've disconnected.

'Well ... I've got an idea.' Casper moves over to my sofa, collapsing next to me and taking my hand. 'I've been thinking it's time we met in real life, Raven.'

The pounding in my ears makes it hard to concentrate. *Why?* We can't meet in real life. They'll see I'm a paraplegic. And that will be the end of everything. I'm not the person I used to be. I can't share in their life of adventure—not anymore. Maybe I should ghost them. If I could find a way to fund my subscription while doing rehab this wouldn't be a problem. The urgency around having to do something would go away. I need to keep this in virtual reality. It's the only place this is possible.

'What if it ...' I search for the right words, 'changes things, meeting in person?'

Casper smiles. 'I hope it does.'

My stomach plummets, and everything goes numb.

'I mean, not in a good way.'

'But we get along so well. I'm sure it would translate to real life. It feels real to me.'

I should say something.

'I guess.'

'We need to do something before your trial ends. Text chat isn't enough for me. Is it for you?'

Why can't I just tell them? This won't end well.

'Okay, I'll meet you. Where?'

'How about a picnic in a park?'

Which park? Where in the park? Will it be accessible? I really have to say something.

'I'm not really ... fond of parks. Any other ideas?'

'There's a café on the corner of Denny and Crowe. Pastry Gods.'

Better.

'Okay.'

'I'll be waiting there tomorrow at 2 pm, sitting at a table in a red jacket, with two croissants, because I know it's your favourite pastry.'

'See you tomorrow.'

I approach the entrance of the café in my wheelchair but can't bring myself to enter. My stupidity at not speaking up overwhelms me. So many late-night chats about exciting adventures we've had, places we've been and everything we'd love to do—I was lying. We've built our whole relationship to this point on a cascade of lies. Me wheeling myself into this café is going to show the ugly truth lurking at the bottom of it all. This is going to change everything. One little omission created this massive problem and I have to face it now. I force myself to enter.

A person with a red jacket sits in the back corner. Two croissants on the table, waiting. Casper—in the flesh. It's awkward to navigate through the other patrons to get to them—but I manage. When I'm beside the table, Casper doesn't even look up from the book in their hands. A crippling pain surges through my chest when I realise, they're waiting for someone who can plant their backside in the chair across from them.

'Hey Casper.'

That gets their attention.

'Raven?' Disbelief.

'Mm-hm.'

The hurt in their eyes is unmistakable—the betrayal. This feels like hello and goodbye. I shouldn't have expected any less. As the silence extends, the urge to leave becomes overwhelming.

My body shrinks into the wheelchair. This was a mistake. 'Sorry, should I go?'

'No. Please don't.' They shake their head, as if caught in a daze. 'I'm just surprised, the way you talked, I was expecting—' Casper gestures at my legs.

I sigh. 'Until recently, they worked fine. Then I had the car accident ... and they stopped working. I'm still adjusting to this new normal. I should have said something.'

Casper gets up and removes the chair before guiding my wheelchair into the spot at the table. 'It's okay. I bet it's a massive adjustment.' Hands rest on my shoulders. 'Sorry if I made you feel like it was a problem.' Casper leans down so their lips brush against my ear. 'It's not. I enjoy your company, more than anything.' They glide back into their own seat and grin at me. I can't help but reciprocate—it must be contagious. I savour my croissant almost as much as I savour the conversation. Wash it

69

down with a couple of cappuccinos while the conversation flows like water over the next few hours. As easy as it was online— easier, really—because now the giant, gaping secret between us has evaporated.

When I need to leave, we make our way to the footpath outside, Casper has a proposition that will enable us to keep seeing each other. Reluctantly, I agree to it. They lean down and hesitate. A question and an invitation. Casper locks eyes with mine and a warmth expands through me creating an overwhelming urge to be closer to them. I lean forward in my chair. They tilt down and peck me on the lips then pause, as if checking in. I reach up and kiss them back, this time it's longer—and mutual. Every nerve ending that wasn't severed in the accident screams for more, but I resist and pull back down into my chair. Casper stumbles, losing their balance as they step back from the chair.

'Wow. Remember, you said you had to go. I don't want you to be late.'

'Until next time?' Always a question.

The smile that extends across their face is almost answer enough on its own, but they still reply, 'Of course.'

At home, my hands keep slipping and I bump into things with my chair, I can't steady myself as I try to navigate to the computer room. It should be fine. Casper offered. What does it mean though? Letting someone do something so generous for me. I log into *The Guest Room*. A notification says my trial subscription has been upgraded to Ultimate through Gift Services. There's a message from Casper telling me it's just a little gift and thank you for meeting them today. When our avatars load into our new Guest Room it's no longer the monochrome sadness of the Basic Environment. Instead, we're inside a luxury rainforest lodge with waterfall views. A large white sofa is facing a fireplace in our Guest Room. It's huge to cater for extra furniture packs. One wall even has doors for extra room add-on packs.

'This is amazing.'

'I know.' Casper grins. 'And it's only the beginning. Wait until you get the package in the mail. Things might be challenging in the real world for you right now, but anything is possible here.'

'But wouldn't you rather be having adventures out in the real world with someone who isn't holding you back?'

'You're not forcing me to be anywhere I don't want to be. I prefer the company right here, whether that's in here or out there.'

EYE OF THE STORM

jeanette o'hagan

Tembei steadied her stance on the water-slick deck. Grey gulls whirled among the masts of the fishing tjung, silver flecks against the charcoal clouds. Bruised waves shed white streamers and a strong south-easterly whipped her hair across her cheeks. Each erratic gust brought the tantalising scents of verdant jungle with the tang of salt and seaweed.

The heady smell of home.

Except for the unsettling overlay of gunpowder and smoke.

This small outpost was not New Hope Harbour, not her home.

Scarred by a recent pirate raid, like her home. Several buildings smouldered, and the seawall wore the scars of cannon balls. Weary villagers cleared rubble, and repaired smashed roofs and walls.

But not defeated and emptied of people like her home had been months earlier.

She blinked back the sting of tears. No time for that. She saved her brothers. Now she must ask a ship of the Legate, to get to New Danton and warn her uncle of the coming pirate attack.

Across the bay, a long boat pulled away from the jetty, the muscular backs of the green-skinned sailors straining at the oars. In the bow, a young Rolan officer stood straight and tall, one booted foot on the gunwale, a hand resting on the hilt of his sword. His peaked hat displayed the intwined golden leaves of a tribune.

Tembei's pulse quickened. Something seemed familiar about the tilt of the young officer's head and his athletic stance. She hurried towards the port side of the ship, where Captain Ikan and first mate stood, ready to receive the Legate's envoy.

The Rishan captain turned and bowed. 'Worthy Tembei.' He tugged at his grey beard and nodded to the long boat skimming towards them. 'You will be safe among your people.'

Tembei returned the bow. 'Many thanks for your help, Captain.' Though he was a Rishan like the pirates, she meant it. After long harsh days at sea in the open tender, the sight of his fishing boat had appeared like a vision of heaven.

A winged shadow glided over the deck, Rajiah, a koraki swooped and landed on her shoulder. He nuzzled her neck and chirruped. A flood of bright images of the settlement and the surrounding jungle tumbled into Tembei's mind; people repairing the villages, soldiers strengthening the fortifications, small creatures scurrying through rice fields and food gardens, but no sign of pirates hiding in the secluded bay.

Tembei's shoulders relaxed. 'Safe for now.'

Captain Ikan nodded. 'Your ordeal is over. Once you are in the Legate's care, we'll head for the Ralakka straits to fill our holds.'

The closer the long boat came with each oar stroke, the harder it became to ignore the piercing stare and commanding figure of the young tribune.

With a heave of a wayward wave, the smaller boat scrapped the side of the fishing tjung. A sailor threw up a hawser and the first mate fastened it to a cleat.

The tribune cupped his mouth. 'Permission to come aboard, Captain.'

'Granted, Honoured Tribune.'

At a flick of the captain's fingers, sailors threw a rope ladder down to the long boat. The tribune shimmied up the heaving side of the ship. Four soldiers followed close behind.

The tribune vaulted on the deck. 'Where are these castaways, Captain?'

Tembei stepped forward. 'My brothers are recovering below deck, Tribune.'

His intense dark gaze smashed against hers. He seemed at once as familiar as her own brothers and yet as unknown as a stranger. His name, his family connection, his clade eluded her.

'Worthy Kwan Tembei, daughter of Kwan Jenri.' He bowed. 'Legate Moi sends his greetings.'

He knew her.

'And you are?'

'Tribune Zu Rarmo. In the service of Commander Legate Moi of the Kato clade.' His voice, rich as tamarind chocolate, held a bitter aftertaste.

Her cheeks warmed. 'Rarmo?' Surely this wasn't her inseparable childhood companion—until his family left New Hope unexpectedly four years ago. Now she detected the slender, laughing lad in this taut, muscular stranger. 'Heaven sent you. New Danton is in great danger. We must send warning without delay.'

Rarmo turned and ordered, 'Captain Ikan, the Imperial Legate hereby commandeers your ship and crew to convey him to New Danton. We sail by tomorrow's morning high tide.'

'Sir! My holds are empty. This will ruin me.'

'Do you question the Legate's orders?'

Captain Ikan's face greyed. 'No, sir. I am loyal.'

'Surely this is not necessary?' Tembei said. 'One of your ships—'

'Do you see ships at our docks?' Rarmo swept his hand towards dark shadows in the water. 'We repelled the pirate raid, but all our ships were sunk. It is vital the Legate informs the Governor.' He shot a smouldering glare at her. 'But you knew that.'

'What do you mean?'

'Reports of your activities reached our outpost, hours before our lookout spotted the pirate tjungs.'

'Activities?'

'Consorting with pirates. Becoming one of them.' He glared at her newly pierced ears. 'How could you betray your own people?'

Tembei's heart thudded hard. 'I had no choice. They took us captive. I ... we escaped to warn you of their plans as soon as we could.'

'That tale would be more believable, if you weren't in intimate company with the notorious Pirate King, Garak Malang. By order of the Legate, you and your brothers will be restrained and questioned. You will face the council's judgment at New Danton.'

She'd worry about proving her innocence after she'd alerted her uncle of the imminent pirate attack on New Danton.

'Opto restrain the prisoner. Take her to the brig,' Rarmo ordered.

This implacable tribune was not the youth she once knew.

The Opto advanced towards her with iron shackles dangling from rough hands. Memories of the tight confinement, the blinding darkness, the putrid smells of her early days on the pirate ship flooded her mind.

Rajiah uncurled, his neck-feathers and fur bridled, his fire-hot anger building.

'Worthy Tribune, is that necessary?' Captain Ikan sputtered. 'The Lady—'

'The Lady stands accused of consorting with the Emperor's implacable enemy. The Legate insists she be restrained.'

'Then do it.' Tembei thrust out her wrists.

The Opto snapped on the iron cuffs, the hard metal biting into her skin.

Captain Ikan tugged his beard. 'She can be confined in her cabin.'

Rarmo grunted. 'You will be held responsible if she escapes.'

'Don't worry, Tribune Zu.' Tembei made her voice bone-freezing cold as the darkest depths of the ocean trenches. 'I have no intention of escaping.'

The next morning, Tembei dragged herself out of bed, shackles at her wrists as heavy as her night-time worries. Dawn light seeped through the shuttered window. Moving water chuckled against the hull. Wind played a xylophone of sounds in the rigging of the baton-ridged sails.

Bare feet thumped the deck in time to the sailors' rhythmic work-chant. The ship was underway.

Rajiah's urgent hunger-images stirred her own. She fetched the food tray inside the door and divided the rice balls, pickled vegetables and boiled egg between them.

Tembei ran her fingers through her chin-length hair and smoothed down her borrowed dress. What if Moi stopped her from seeing her uncle. She needed to warn him of the dangers they faced. Taking a stylus from the desk, she inked it and wrote a few words.

Shadows shifted across the room, ripples of light playing on the low ceiling. Rarmo's stern face invaded her thoughts. The clench of his jaw, flex of his muscular physique, and the flash of betrayal in his dark koi-shaped eyes. So different from the youth she knew. She'd missed him terribly. Soon after he left her parents were killed.

Rajiah fluttered down. She tickled him under the chin. 'Then, I found you.'

Now Rarmo worked for Legate Moi, her uncle's greatest rival.

A rap on the cabin door punctured her thoughts. Rajiah flew on leathery wings back to the beam.

The two soldiers burst into the cramped space and flanked the door, followed by Rarmo. He brought the aroma of sun-warmed wood, salt-laden wind, and denied freedom.

'Worthy Kwan Tembei, you have all you need?'

'If life can be reduced to cold food and confinement.' Despite her quickening pulse, Tembei matched his cool, indifferent tone.

'Good.' He glanced at the smeared sheet of bamboo-paper and raised his brows. 'A confession?'

Tembei scowled at this friend-turned-enemy. 'My brothers, how are they?'

'Safe.' Ramo folded his arms. 'Did they know of your treacherous scheme?'

'What scheme? To escape the pirates?'

His lips flattened. 'Did you give Grak Malang details of troop numbers and defences before the attacks on the outposts?'

'No! Why would I destroy my own home?'

'Because you are Malang's paramour.'

'His what?' Tembis smothered a laugh. Clearly, Moi or her mysterious accuser did not know Grak's secret. The pirate king was a woman. A formidable woman with hidden depths, even compassion, but ruthless nonetheless.

'Find that amusing?'

'Hardly. Why would we have chanced the open ocean in a tender except to escape Malang? We could've perished, if the good captain had not found us.'

Doubt flickered in Rarmo's dark eyes, to be replaced by deep anger. He leant over her. 'To trick us, so your lover can expel the Rolan from the Archipelago.'

'I escaped to warn our people. Is this so hard to believe? You condemn me before hearing my story and chain me like a slave, just as the pirates did.' She lifted her arms, the iron links clashing together like old regrets.

'Our witness says otherwise.'

'The Kato are a rival clade. Someone could be trying to discredit us.'

'This is useless!' He turned to go.

'Worthy Tribune Zu. Rarmo. Please. At least remove the chains.'

His jaw flexed. 'Hold still,' he growled and fished the key from his brocaded jacket. She felt his body-warmth, saw the pulse in his throat. Her heart tapped a traitorous rhythm.

The iron bracelets clicked open.

'You are too kind.' Her breathless words lacked the sarcastic sting she intended.

His thumb brushed over the fading scars on her wrists. 'How did you get these?'

'Where do you think? From the pirate's shackles.'

He dropped her hands like scorched rocks. 'Is that all your worthiness requires?' He backed towards the door.

'Tribune Zu, might I walk the decks each day for a breath of fresh air?'

Rarmo's expression softened. 'I will take your request to the Legate.'

Tembei paced between her bunk to the door and back again for the hundredth time that day. Apart from the regular delivery of food and fresh linens, no one had visited her cabin, not even to interrogate her about her supposed treachery.

She pressed her face against the salt-smeared porthole and squinted at the dark vastness beyond. Pearlescent dawn light lined the ever-moving horizon. Small islands jutted out of watery plains. How much longer before they arrived in New Danton?

With a crash of boots, the cabin door slammed open.

She spun around and glared at the intruder. 'I want to speak to that mealy-mouthed Tribune.'

'Then you have your wish, Worthy.'

A stalwart figure in a blue coat stood in the middle of cabin. 'Rarmo … Tribune Zu.'

He bowed, stiff-backed and unsmiling. 'The Legate agreed to one hour on the deck at dawn and dusk.'

'It's been six days.'

He raised an eyebrow. 'You can spend the allotted time grumbling or take the opportunity.'

He was right.

'Escort me to the deck, Tribune.'

Rajiah glided from his perch and landed on her shoulder, sending excited thoughts of hunting fish. In return, she impressed on him the need to scout the surrounding areas.

The corners of Rarmo's eyes softened. A crack in the armour.

She took his arm. He did not pull away. The feel of hard muscle and the fine weave of his shirt beneath her fingers felt right. His familiar scent left her breathless.

'This way, Worthy, careful on the stairs.'

The stairs were the least of her problems when her thoughts scattered like startled seagulls into a stormy wind.

This morning's promenade along the deck lingered beyond the allotted hour despite the blustery day and choppy seas. Tembei placed a hand on the low rail to steady herself. Three days had passed since the Legate agreed to these fleeting moments in the sun. What if Grak Malang had reached Ba-tang? How long before that small outpost fell, and the pirates marched across the isthmus to attack New Danton? To distract from the ever-circling thoughts, Tembei sought out Rajiah soaring over a nearby island. Below him a white-ruffled river tumbled over a cliff into a fern-fringed pond. She inhaled the rich, loamy scent of the jungle, felt the silky water sliding over her skin.

'What do you see, to conjure such a beautiful smile?'

It took a second to realise Rarmo's words came from beside her and not the distant past.

She hitched a shoulder. 'Remember that day we half-drowned in the Nori rapids.'

His mouth twitched. 'A mishap I prefer to forget.'

Sudden anger flared. 'Is that why you never replied to my letters?'

His face hardened to basalt. 'I received no letters from you, Worthy.'

'I sent them. Every ten-day, for years.' Her lips twisted. 'You said you loved me, then abandoned me.'

'I abandoned you?' His nostrils flared. 'Your uncle sacked my father, unjustly accused him of cheating, threw our family out of New Hope, threatened him if we … I … ever to returned to Kwan lands or saw you again.'

Tembei blinked. 'My uncle?'

Could Uncle have done such a thing? The sun played catch-me-if-you-can behind the towering clouds. A storm approached; she could taste it in the wind.

'Rarmo, I did not betray our promise. Nor have I betrayed our people.'

A sudden tilt of the deck untethered her feet. She flailed her arms, her fingers scrapping the rails. The tarred planks hurtled towards her.

Strong arms caught her. Enveloped in a heady smell of sandalwood, her face pressed against his brocade coat. His heartbeats drummed in tune with her own rapid beat. For a moment the two of them stood cocooned against the world.

Then they both jumped apart as though stung by scorpions.

'I ...' Her cheeks flamed.

He cleared his throat. 'I should return you to the cabin, Worthy.'

'I need to call Rajiah.'

She gripped the railing and reached out for the fierce, free koraki-mind. Rajiah skimmed over the restless waves, belly full of fresh-caught fish. *Come back, little one.* Rajiah snapped his jaws, resisting the call to return to the cabin-prison. *Storm is building. Come now,* she urged.

A gust of wind and rain splattered over the ship, wetting her cheeks. Sailors scurried about securing loose items and furling the main sail.

'Tribune, get Worthy Tembei below deck,' Captain Ikan roared. 'Your soldiers too. The Legate commands us to shelter in Hidden Bay until the storm passes.'

Rarmo touched her elbow. 'Come, Tembei.'

The erratic movements of the tjung slowed their pace to tortoise-speed. The prow of the ship turned towards the strait between the bigger island and a group of smaller ones. A larger wave crested and sloshed over the deck.

She mind-touched Rajiah. He flew towards them over the sweep of a wide bay in the embrace of the densely forested slopes of a tall volcano. Close to the sandy shore, a tjung bobbed at anchor on the choppy water.

Tembei's heart seized, then galloped away at an insane beat. Her feet stopped moving. Black sails, Rishan sea-god pennant. Pirates. Waiting in ambush. Their small fishing tjung would be outgunned.

The wind dropped. An eerie silence settled over the ship. She raised her eyes to the nearest island, bruised storm clouds roiling skyward above the cone of a dormant volcano. A stray sunbeam streamed through a gap and caught the emerald and sapphire wings of the koraki flying towards her. The wind picked up. Rain pelted down.

'Tembei.' Rarmo tugged at her arm. 'You will be safe in your cabin.'

'No! We must warn the captain. A pirate fighting tjung lurks in Hidden Bay.'

Rarmo's eyes narrowed. 'Is this a ploy? How could you know that!'

Rajiah dropped out of the sky and landed on her shoulder. His golden eyes slitted at the Tribune.

Rarmo would think her mad if she told the truth, but she already stood accused of treason. And that pirate tjung would destroy them.

'Tembei, answer me.'

'I ... I can see through Rajiah's eyes. When he flew over the big island, I saw a fighting tjung flying the pirate pennant.'

Rarmo stared at her.

'I'm not crazy. We have to tell the Captain, before it is too late.'

He puffed out his cheeks and smiled. 'You always had a way with animals, but a beast-speaker?'

The ship shuddered and bucked as it crossed into the straits. Tembei gripped his strong hands in her own. 'Please, Rarmo, we must warn Captain Ikan.'

'No. The Legate gave the order. Only he can rescind it. Come.' He hooked his arm into hers and steered her towards the stern cabin.

The Legate Moi. Her uncle's greatest rival and her accuser. Dread weighed down her stomach like ballast in a sinking ship.

'Tribune, why is this traitor blotting my vision?' Legate Moi's blade-sharp voice sent shivers down Tembei's spine. The tall, elegant man had changed little apart from the sprinkling of salt at his temples.

'Honourable Legate,' Rarmo bowed low. 'Worthy Tembei has news that, with respect, you should hear.'

The Legate's sharp nose creased. 'This traitor can say nothing I would wish to hear.'

Rarmo's cheeks purpled. 'Sir, this goes to the safety of the ship.'

Moi flicked his manicured fingers at Tembei. 'Speak your lies.'

Tembei swallowed against the sea-grit lodged in her throat. 'Honourable Legate, a pirate fighting tjung awaits within Hidden Bay ready to strike.'

The Legate pinned her with his gaze. 'And you know this, how?'

'My koraki saw the pirates as he flew over the bay.'

The Legate erupted into laughter. 'You think me a fool? You plan to deny us safe harbour!'

A jagged silver line split the confusion of dark sea and sky in the large window behind him.

'No!' Tembei retrieved the image of Grak's navigational charts. 'There is another bay on a smaller isle north-west of here.'

'Where, no doubt, your lover Malang will attack us. Enough! Tie her to the mast.'

A mighty rumble of thunder shook the cabin. Tembei's skin prickled. To be tied to the mast in the middle of the storm?

The ship lurched and tilted as though changing direction. A rain-darkened headland loomed like a crouching tiger.

Too late to turn back.

'I gave you an order, Tribune.'

85

Rarmo bowed. 'Sir!' He steered Tembei out into the raging storm.

Rain lashed Tembei's face. Forested headlands, shrouded by mist and driving torrents loomed on both sides of the fishing tjung. Choppy charcoal water widened into a sheltered bay. Tembei seethed at how easily Rarmo had complied to the Legate's outrageous order.

Rarmo leant closer, his warmth soaking into her side. He shouted over the roar of winds and waves. 'Are you sure you saw a fighting ship, not a trader?'

She glared at him. 'Yes!'

'Right.' He signalled to a soldier hurrying past. 'Send word. Ready the cannon and our men to fight off a pirate attack.'

'Yes, sir.'

'And free and arm the prisoners if they will stand with us.'

The guard's eyes popped. 'Sir? The Legate ...'

'Are you questioning my orders?'

''No, sir.' The soldier sped away.

'You are freeing my brothers?'

Rarmo nodded, the mischievous smile she remembered tugging at his lips. 'We need fighters.'

Tembei threw her arms around him. For a heartbeat, he held her tight and the turmoil of the storm faded.

'Pirate tjung ahead,' the lookout bellowed.

'Go below deck, Tembei.'

'No, Rarmo. I can fight. Or have you forgotten our sword play?'

He grinned, rain streaming down his face, hair flattened, and clothes plastered to his body. 'I remember.' He gave her his cutlass. 'Be careful. I don't want to lose you again.'

The fishing tjung's cannon thundered, its round nozzle spurting fire. A metal ball smashed into the deck of the pirate tjung, splintering wood, scattering enemies. An acrid, sulphurous taste tainted the rain-soaked air. The soldiers lined along the port-side rail discharged their muskets, blue smoke dampened by the driving rain. The pirates returned a volley of musket fire, keeping their canon in reserve. Their ship edged alongside the smaller fishing tjung.

'They intend to board us. To take prisoners.' Tembei tugged Rajiah's drenched fur. 'We need a distraction.'

She sent the image of the baton-ridged sails aflame to Rajiah. Rajiah took to the air with powerful downward strokes and darted towards the pirate ship, smoke curling from his nostrils.

The ships crashed together starboard to portside. Pirates threw grappling hooks. Along the deck, Rarmo and his soldiers fought off the pirates attempting to scramble across the gap while the sailors dislodged the hooks. Her brothers rushed towards the melee, cutlasses raised and fire in their eyes.

Tembei ran to Captain Ikan at the tiller. 'Captain, send sailors with nets to entangle the pirates.'

He nodded to the First Mate. 'Do as Worthy Tembei suggests.'

At first, the nets slowed the pirates clambering aboard, and the sailors stabbed them with boathooks and rigging knives. But the pirates kept coming in waves.

The rain cleared and the sun burst out from behind the clouds, coaxing diamonds from the wrack and ruin on land and sea. The eye of the storm.

A shout erupted on the pirate's tjung. Fierce, ravenous rivers of fire ran up the sails, sending glowing cinders twirling to the deck. Go Rajiah.

Many pirates rushed back to douse the flames. Rarmo and his soldiers pushed the thinning ranks back towards their ship.

A thunderous roar, and a cannon ball hurtled into the central mast of the pirate ship, scattering fire and debris. Fire ran along the tarred deck. Hungry flames leapt higher and higher.

Desperate pirates leapt into the water.

Rarmo waved a cutlass. 'Cut our ship free. Put distance between us.'

Tembei ran towards the closest grappling hook and slashed through the rope. Waves of blistering heat warming her skin. Others joined her, using boat hooks and muskets to push away the burning ship.

The two tjungs drifted apart in the eerie stillness.

Rajiah returned, thrumming his pleasure.

'Tembei, you won the day.'

Tembei turned and sank deep into the dark eyes of the Tribune Zu Rarmo. 'We did.' Joy fizzed beneath her ribs. 'Friends?'

'More than friends. Always.'

A gurgling rush and the pirate ship disappeared beneath the foamy, debris-filled waves. The water slapped over it, then rushed outwards in an ever-widening wave. The ship bucked and they fell into each other.

His arms wrapped around her, and she melted into his embrace. Tilting her head, she pressed her lips to his. He cupped her head and pulled her closer, deepening the kiss until her legs trembled.

He was the one. He'd always been the one.

A thunderous noise erupted around them. She pulled back, keeping hold of Rarmo's strong fingers. Sailors surrounded them, hollering and stamping their feet.

Her older brother, Dengma, strode towards them from one side, the Legate came from the other.

Rarmo tightened his grip on her hand.

Dengma reached them first. 'Sir, let go of my sis ... His eyes widened. 'Rarmo? What happened to you?'

'Long story. But I intend to ask your uncle permission to court your sister.'

Dengma clapped him on the back. 'Took you long enough.'

'Tribune, you are relieved of command,' the Legate roared. His silk robe remained immaculate. Not a hair out of place. Not a single sign of battle.

Rarmo inclined his head. 'I find no honour in serving the Kato clade.'

The Legate swept a hand towards Rarmo, Tembei and her brothers. 'Opto, round up the traitors and put them all in irons.'

'With respect, sir,' the Opto said, 'Were it not for the Tribune Zu, Worthy Kwan and her brothers, we'd all be in pirate chains.'

Captain Ikan nodded. 'They fought with us.'

The Legate swivelled his head. 'The Kwans are accused traitors against the Imperial rule. Seize them, now! Or you will share their fate.'

First Rarmo, now the soldiers dared defy the Legate.

Hope rose like a tide. 'We will face our accuser before the Council, but we must make haste to New Danton, to warn of the coming danger.'

Dengma spread his hands. 'My sister speaks the truth. We face a greater danger than ever before.'

The wind picked up filling the sail. Raindrops splatted on the deck.

'First we must weather the rest of the storm,' Captain Ikan said.

Legate Moi glared at each of them. 'You will all regret this mutiny.' Spinning on his heels, he retreated to his cabin.

Rajiah trumpeted a victory call.

Rarmo wrapped his arm around Tembei's waist. 'We'll face the future together.'

Tembei nestled closer. Whatever challenges lay ahead, she no longer stood isolated and alone.

CONTEMPORARY

ROMANCE

WITHIN THE FIRE

robin adolphs

When twilight fades and fires are lit, I stare enthralled into the flames
Where flickering shadows cast their spell and on my heart lay claim.

And mesmerised by shifting worlds, I dream of love and visualise
A kindred soul and love unchained, reflected in my true one's eyes.

Eagerly, I lean in close. Fire's gentle fingers stroke my face
And hold me safe. Wrapped in the joy of love's embrace.

The fire dies and embers glow. My heart stays warm. It's had a chance
To dare to dream and feel romance.

CHARMS OF LOVE

.

THE WILDERNESS CURE

lea scott

Jess plopped down on a rock, defeated, dropping the camera from her hand. Someone had told her about this rock pool in the forest where platypus families were sometimes seen. She had hoped to get some photos to take back with her. The unusual but endearing creatures would be sure to reinforce their campaign against the greedy developers who wanted to clear a large tract of wilderness nearby for a housing estate. Pyes Creek ran through that land and was a known home to a local paddle of platypuses. So far, the water had not revealed anything to her except for a few floating sticks being twirled by the eddying currents.

The aimless currents reminded Jess of her life, which had recently sent her into a tailspin of her own. She should never have dated someone from her law firm. Career before love. That was her new mantra. It was her own fault that the partners had passed her up for promotion once things turned sour with Gerry.

But the pain was twofold. *He* had got the promotion she had worked so hard for.

She wiped an unwelcome tear from her cheek then looked up to discover she wasn't alone. Through bleary eyes, she watched a man emerge from the trees above, free-climbing down the cliff. As he picked his way down, she found herself mesmerised by his fiery hair, which extended down the sides of his face, hugging his chin in a close-cut beard. As her eyes wandered down his freckled arms, she was awed by the ripple of the muscles in his shoulders, partly exposed in his athletic tank top and shimmering with sweat, despite the brisk air.

As he reached the ground, he turned and met her eye. Her cheeks warmed, feeling like a peeping tom who had been caught out. A quick wink at her and he ran off down the trail.

As Jess drove past the forest on her way into town, she thought about the mysterious man she had encountered the day before. She had always been a sucker for redheads. Maybe that's why things didn't really work out with Gerry with his dark mop of curls. It had to be something in her makeup—only two percent of the population had the gene. Although she and her mother had been born blonde, she had seen photos of her grandfather as a young man. She had only known him as a silver fox but he had sported a superb quiff of red hair in his youth. She pushed the thought away as she parked the car outside the community hall. She had no time for men—redhead or not. She had a much more important reason for being here in this growing hinterland town. She had an environmental cause to fight!

As Jess made her way toward the meeting room, she heard raised voices. The townsfolk were probably eating the developer's representative alive.

What was his name again? She hadn't had time to consult her notes.

'You'll regret this!' a loud voice bellowed as Jess opened the door.

A hush fell over the room, her presence being the only calmness amid the worked-up crowd.

'Here she is now.' The threatening growl came from a woman with a 'told-you-so' look on her face and a purple streak through her grey hair. 'Our environmental lawyer.'

The woman, who she recalled as local activist Mandy Mulligan, grinned at Jess as if she was their saviour. Jess wasn't sure if she was entirely comfortable with that role, but she was sure as hell going to try to save the environmentally sensitive pocket of Pyes Creek from this greedy developer. And just maybe, if she could win this case, the partners back at her city law firm might stop passing her over for promotion.

She stole a quick glance at the object of their wrath, who sat in profile to her position at the entry door, giving her the advantage of taking him in without him being aware. He hadn't even bothered to acknowledge her arrival as he ran his large hand through his rusty coloured hair. His expression was hidden behind a perfectly manicured beard, but she could tell from his stiff body language he was enraged.

That's all she needed. She hoped she could facilitate a meaningful discussion between the developer's representative and the townsfolk. She cursed the roadworks that made her late for the meeting, allowing the townsfolk to already go to town on this unsuspecting man. Not that she felt sorry for him. Anyone involved with Boom Investments and its bid to destroy the environment deserved what came to them. But stirring them up further was only going to make them dig their heels in.

Jess made her way towards the riser that had been set up for the occasion. The man shot her a quick sideways glance. Her mouth dropped. It was *him*. He looked different with his freckled muscles hidden under his long-sleeved business shirt. Behind his anger, there was a momentary plea for help in his eyes. He reminded her of a deer caught in the headlights. Had they prepared him for this onslaught? But as quickly as it came, his expression was masked by hostility.

Jess turned away and addressed the crowd with a shrug of her shoulders. 'I'm so sorry I'm late. Roadworks!'

A hum of acknowledgement rose from the crowd. With the tourism numbers growing in the region, the town was subjected to a constant barrage of road upgrades.

'Let's start over,' Jess continued.

Mandy Mulligan piped up again, repeating what she had already conveyed to the crowd based on their joint sighs.

Jess let the woman's voice fade as she returned her gaze to the man beside her. His hands gesticulated wildly, at times becoming closed fists, as he responded to the crowd. She knew his type. His bullying behaviour. It didn't matter what the townsfolk said, he was never going to agree to their terms. This approach was clearly a waste of time, and it looked like the only avenue left would be to proceed to court.

An hour later, after much too-ing and fro-ing, Jess's opinion had not changed. She packed up her carefully prepared notes, most of which she had not had the opportunity to discuss because the crowd had their own agenda and the loudest voice on the stage had been that of her opponent. As she stood, he stalked past her, knocking her papers to the ground.

'Hey,' she protested. He stopped, looked like he was going to stoop to help. There was that look again, as his hand brushed against her arm. Mandy, who had done much of the protesting, appeared at her side and he seemed to think better of it. 'Go to hell,' he said in a gruff voice as he turned his back on them and exited the room. Jess was taken aback by his lack of professionalism.

'Ignore him love. He'll get his come-uppance in court.'

Jess stood for a long moment, watching the empty space he had left in the doorway. There was a warm spot on her arm where he had touched it. The heat moved up her body and found a place somewhere deeper inside her. She flicked her arm several times to shake off the uninvited feeling, then stooped to help Mandy pick up her scattered papers.

Ignoring the *No Trespassing* signs, Jess pushed through the undergrowth, cursing as the branches flexed then snapped back and slapped her in the face. As a lawyer, it was not her habit to break the law. But after yesterday's unproductive meeting, she had to find out what was happening for herself if she was to make a case against Boom Investments. The town depended on her and she didn't want to let them down—or herself.

The developers had electrified the fences around the rest of the property, so the only approach was to cross the creek. She had underestimated how dense the bush would be on this side of the property. Now her shoes squelched water and midges attacked her bare arms with their ferocious bites. She was about to give up and try to come up with a different approach when she heard splashing. She edged closer to the creek bank and was surprised to see a platypus careening through the water. Another one joined it, and they ducked and chased each other in circles. From her research on the animals, she knew this was their mating ritual. This was what the development endangered. She snapped photos of their delightful antics on her phone.

A sharp crack echoed through the trees. Jess pushed on through the branches, even more determined.

Crack! There it was again. It sounded close.

Light filtered through the thinning canopy, revealing slivers of blue sky above. Jess stopped short of the tree line, taking cover behind one of the huge rough-barked trunks of a bunya pine. The townsfolk informed her that the bunyas held great significance for the local indigenous people. Although she did suspect they brought this information to her attention because it benefited their cause more than they cared about the value of country to its original inhabitants. She made a mental note to connect with the local indigenous elder to build her case about the loss of the magnificent trees.

From her safe place, she spied the red-headed man from the meeting the night before. He lifted an axe above his head, then powered it down into the trunk of a large sapling. He was clearing the trees. *Illegally!* She had managed to get an injunction to stop the clearing until an environmental assessment was done on the impact on the local flora and fauna. The machines were at rest, but she was appalled at these sneaky tactics.

Jess stormed out from her hiding spot, ready to confront him. She jumped as there was another splintering crack, then the light above her turned to shadow.

'Look out!'

It was too late. The sapling came hurtling towards her as it fell from its standing position. She tried to race sideways but she could not outrun the sprawling branches. She felt a sharp pain and looked down to see blood spurting from a deep gash in her left calf. Her head felt woozy. As she slipped from consciousness, she realised she'd taken a hard hit to her crown.

Jess squeezed her eyes open, wincing as a severe pain shot through her head. She closed her eyes again, groaning. An antiseptic smell reached her nostrils, and she could hear the rattling of trays and beeps of machines around her. She opened her eyes again, this time more slowly. A face swam into her blurry vision. She waited for her eyes to adjust.

'You!'

'I'm so sorry,' he said. 'I didn't mean for anyone to get hurt.' There was an unexpected gentleness in his voice.

'What the hell are you doing in here?' an older man shouted as he appeared in the doorway.

Jess closed her eyes again, and the next time she opened them she was alone in the room. The window revealed the setting sun as dusk approached. A nurse placed a cuff around her arm and shoved a thermometer in her mouth. She tried to talk, but the nurse shooshed her until she had removed and read the instrument.

'Good,' she announced.

'How long have I been here?' Jess asked.

'Just since yesterday morning,' the nurse replied. 'We had to keep you sedated for a bit while that swelling on your head went down.'

Jess reached up and felt the prick of stitches in the top of her head. A small patch was shaved, but her long hair would cover that. She was more concerned that two days were lost—how could that be? She looked around the room for some kind of answer.

'Don't worry, that young man of yours said he would be back soon. He just went to get a coffee. Lovely chap. You're very lucky.' She winked as she left the room.

Young man of mine. Who was she talking about? Had Gerry heard about her accident? He was the last person she wanted here, handing out false sympathy.

Her question was answered as the man who had caused her injuries entered the room with a takeaway coffee cup in his hand. She glared at him as her lip formed into an involuntary snarl.

'Okay, I guess I deserve that look. But I really am sorry.' He dropped his cup on the wheeled tray and extended his open palms towards her. 'I'm Rudy, by the way. Just in case you're still a bit foggy.'

Jess raised her eyebrows.

'I know. I've heard it all before. You can imagine how mercilessly I was teased at school. With a name like that—*and* red hair. Rudy the Ranga.'

Jess sensed the pain behind the admission. Sympathy flowed through her chest—until she remembered who this man worked for! In her post-sedation state, she had a hard time reconciling the two thoughts.

'You work for Boom Investments?' was all she managed to say.

'Yes.' His eyes dropped. 'It's my father's company,' he said, as if it was enough of an explanation.

In response to her expectant glare, he continued, 'I think he expected my sister would come on board. She's always been his favourite—and much more cutthroat than me. But she's off making a career of being an Olympic athlete. My father is getting on. It just fell on me to step up and take on the family business.'

'But how can you support what he's doing here? And why were you cutting down those trees?'

'You don't know my father. He insisted, and he's not someone you can say no to.'

Through the blur of the past two days, Jess remembered the older man shouting at Rudy through the hospital door.

'Do you want to say no?'

Rudy nodded, and she saw the sincerity in his eyes. His hand lay on the bed beside her, and she took it in hers. 'I do. I never really thought much about the environment. I just followed my father's wishes blindly. But you've made me see things differently. I did take in what you said at that meeting, you know.' He picked up a bound booklet from the chair. 'And while you've been laying here, I read your report.'

Jess's cheeks warmed. 'Let's do it together then.'

She convinced herself she said that because it would be good to have an ally on the inside. It could help her to win her case. But she couldn't deny her heart was racing as she held his hand.

The next evening, Jess and Rudy sat opposite each other in a dark corner of a local restaurant. It was mid-week, so she knew most of the townsfolk were at home and the few patrons seemed to be travellers passing through. She didn't want anyone to think she was cavorting with the enemy. Her head had cleared, despite a niggling pain from the stitches under her hair and those in her calf. She was focused on coming up with a plan to ensure that if the development happened, it would at least happen in an eco-friendly way.

'So do you think you'll be able to talk your father into some kind of compromise?' she asked Rudy.

'I'm sure going to try,' he said as he lifted his glass in a toast. As their glasses clinked, his gaze penetrated deep into her eyes and her stomach flittered. It was a long time since she had a reaction like this to anyone. Not even Gerry stirred her up in the way Rudy did since that first moment in the forest. She'd never believed in love at first sight.

But maybe ...

Jess checked her thoughts. There was more at stake here. *Focus*.

Rudy reached across the table. His fingertips lingered on hers, almost as if he was asking permission. When she returned his warm smile, he took her hand fully in his as he continued to map out a plan to convince his father to slow down. Jess didn't hear his words. She was too intent on watching how his lips moved. The sound that came from them was like a drug. Deep in tone. Compassionate in nature. How could this man be involved in a project that could cause such wanton destruction to the environment?

Loyalty. He was loyal to his family. That was a good trait, wasn't it? Even if, in this case, it led to unintended consequences. He assured her he did care about the trees, and the platypuses. By the end of the evening, she was sure he would come through for her—and for them.

She glanced at her watch. It was only 8.30 pm but they were the only patrons left in the restaurant. The owner glared at them in a friendly but firm way indicating he wanted to go home, and so should they. She took the final sip of her wine, then stood and followed Rudy to the register. She pulled out her credit card at the same time he did.

'No, I've got this,' he said placing a hand on her shoulder. 'I always pay when I take a lady out.'

Jess could feel the tingle from his touch moving from her shoulder all the way down to her toes. There was definitely electricity between them. Is that what he considered this was? Taking her out? The tingle turned into a glow.

A cold breeze hit them as they exited the warmth of the restaurant. A shock to her system, she ran her hands up and down her arms as goosebumps developed. She should have known to bring something warmer with her. The nights could be considerably cooler up here on the range. Rudy didn't miss a beat as he took off his jacket and placed it around her shoulders. He drew her towards him and embraced her shivering body.

'There. Is that better?'

She burrowed into his chest. 'Mmmm, yes it is. Thank you.'

He wrapped his arm around her waist and walked her towards her car. When they stopped, he gazed into her eyes and his hand moved to her cheek. He stroked it with soft fingers.

'I'll do my best to make sure it goes well tomorrow. I promise.'

His words brought Jess back to reality. The court case. She had to be on her best form. She stepped back, took off his jacket and handed it to him.

'I better get moving. It's going to be a big day.'

Later that night, she recalled the look of disappointment in his eyes as she drifted into a restless sleep.

Things did not go their way in court. Rudy had tried his best, but the injunction was overturned due to lack of *satisfactory* evidence. The day the investigators went out to the creek, the weather was wild and the platypuses were sheltering unseen. Even so, Jess thought they had produced more than enough evidence, including her photos of the mating ritual. She didn't understand it. Clearly the head of Boom Investments had influence. Money talked.

Her phone buzzed. A loud drone made it difficult to hear the caller. 'You'll have to speak up.'

A familiar voice shouted, 'Mandy Mulligan.' Jess braced herself, expecting an earful of abuse. Instead, the voice delivered an impassioned plea.

'The machines have started up again. We're here right now and we're going to stop them. We hoped you'd join us.'

'What do you mean, you're going to stop them? Is it safe?'

'Safety in numbers,' Mandy replied. 'We're going to chain ourselves to the trees. We've already called the media.'

Jess flinched. If someone got hurt, it would be her fault. She'd given them hope then let them down. She grabbed her car keys and dashed for the door.

When Jess arrived at the scene, it was bedlam. Police cars were lined up along the front of the property. A group of protesters strutted back and forth with crudely painted placards denouncing Boom Investments with loud chants. In the background, some of the trees had been felled but the large machinery had come to a halt. Mandy and another grey-haired gent had carried through with their threat and were chained to two big bunya pines. At a nearby media truck Mandy was shouting into the microphone a journalist held up to her face.

But the thing that shocked Jess the most was the sight of Rudy standing alongside his father, who was shoving and shouting at the protesters. She stormed towards him.

'I thought you were on my side!' she screamed, then turned on her heels to join the picketers.

'Wait.'

Jess ignored him as she picked up a discarded placard. She thrust the sign into the air and waved it in front of the television cameras, joining the chant from the united group. When she dared to look back, Rudy still stood by his father. Anger coursed through her veins. She was stupid to believe anything he'd said.

He'd played her all along.

Jess was absorbed by the evening television news coverage of the protest. The program was disrupted by a loud knock on the door. When she saw Rudy standing outside, she attempted to slam the door but he was too quick. He placed his steel-capped boot in the gap. She thrust her shoulder against the door, but it wouldn't shut.

'Jess, please just let me explain.'

She shoved the door harder, but it still wouldn't budge. She stood back defeated and let him enter.

'I don't want to hear anything you have to say.' Her shoulders slumped.

'Oh, I think you might,' he said with a grin.

'You think this is funny?' she screamed. 'You think killing innocent animals and trees is *funny*?'

'Of course not.'

'Then how could you stand there and support him? Support what they were doing?' She moved into the kitchen, placing the bench between herself and Rudy in case she acted on her desire to slap him.

'Do you think that is what I was doing? I wasn't. I was just trying to protect an old man who was getting himself in too deep. He is still my father, no matter what you think of him.'

'Like father, like son I guess.' Her venomous tone displayed no empathy.

He shifted to her side of the bench so that she had no way to get away from him. He edged up and gripped her by the shoulders. 'Is that really what you think?'

The hint of sadness in his eyes threw her for a moment. She ignored it, letting her head take precedence over her heart.

'Yes, that's exactly what I think.'

His voice softened. 'Well, you're wrong. And I'm going to prove it to you.'

He let go and pulled a piece of paper from his pocket, waving it in front of her.

'What's that,' she snarled, unable to let go of her irritation.

'My father and I have had a long chat. We think it's time that he took some time out to enjoy life. He has signed the company over to me.' He waited for her to react.

Jess felt herself letting her guard down a little. 'So that means ...'

'That means, like I said, that I am going to prove it to you. From tomorrow, the machines are on hold until we can find a better way to protect the wilderness.'

Excitement welled up inside her and raced down her arms, giving them a mind of their own. They thrust out and wrapped around Rudy's neck in an enthusiastic embrace.

'We're going to need a good environmental lawyer if I want to take the company in a new eco-friendly direction,' he whispered into her ear.

Rudy held her tight. She turned her face upwards. He stroked her hair as his face moved closer to hers. This time she didn't pull away. As their lips connected, she realised this was the remedy she needed. The promotion at the city law firm no longer seemed to matter, as the world she had once desired faded away.

FLOYD JACKSON IS DEAD

emma rennison

Friday

A bulging rucksack knocks me, flattening my face against the person in front. Natalie dips her head to check. I nod. I'm okay. Somewhere down the train carriage, a group of girls burst into 'Not Just Anyone' and the lyrics sweep through the crowd like a Mexican wave. A high-pitched beep sounds and the doors glide open. Everyone rushes forward and we tumble onto the platform in a giant mass of multicoloured Doc Martens.

Outside the station I'm handed the *Evening Gazette*, the headline oversized, like it's shouting the weather forecast. *Hot! Hot! Hot!*

'Soph?' Nat holds out her hand and we link up on autopilot, like we do at every gig. 'Good to go?'

'Yep.' I readjust my bag strap. My hip aches, but today, I don't care.

We join the trail of other backpack-clad teens, their favourite bands displayed across their chests like proud beacons. A row of oversized ants all heading to the same final destination. The entrance to the Bank Holiday Weekend Rock Festival.

'So he knows you're going?' I turn my head to Nat as the line slows for tickets to be shown and wristbands to be clipped.

'Yeah. I mentioned we'd be here during every class.'

'We *will* make this happen.' I grin, wishing I had a speck of her confidence.

'Best wingman ever.' Nat squeezes me into her.

We're funnelled towards separate turnstiles and I unzip my crossbody bag and pull out a rectangular card, perforated on one side with a fine broken line. It's one blemish, a tiny hole where it was pinned to my corkboard. The ticket for what I already know will be the best summer of my life—August 1995.

Natalie is scanned and wristbanded first. She glances over at me, her forearm in the air like she's just left a Saturday detention. The pink plastic strap secured above her collection of embroidered friendship bracelets. As she shuffles forward her rucksack catches in the gateway, trapping her between the prongs. A laugh bursts from her as she's untangled.

I push through, the cool metal pressing against my stomach as it clicks over, and I'm in. Over the threshold. Officially a citizen of this amazing new world.

'Nat!' A male voice calls out and I raise my head to peer over her shoulder.

'Is it?' she asks, and grabs at my elbow as I confirm it is.

She spins around, her braid swinging with her, to face him. Simon Taylor. Tall with a mop of messy strawberry-blond hair flicked at the side by a cowlick that matches his dimple. It's clear why she likes him.

He dives through two small groups and stops in front of us, hands on hips as he catches his breath. 'I'd know your laugh anywhere.'

She beams at him and he mirrors it, wrapping her in a giant bear hug.

As they break away, two others appear next to him. A guy, sun-kissed freckled skin with waved dark hair that insists on falling over one side of his face despite him brushing it back with his palm. And a girl, a whole head taller than me, with the most perfect thick golden mane.

'I can't believe we've found each other.' Simon grabs at his friend. 'Ben, this is Natalie.'

'Nice to meet you at last.' Ben shakes her hand and turns to me, his arm outstretched. His dark chestnut eyes lock onto mine and it's like there's a sudden surge in gravity and my whole body leans towards him. As our fingers brush, his mouth twists into a half-grin. 'Great hat.'

My fingers flutter to the rim as if I've just remembered it's there.

'This is Sophie.' Natalie puts her hand around my waist. Ben's smile lifts higher, crinkling the corners of his eyes, and my heart skips a little faster.

'I'm Bec.' The blonde girl announces. Simon glances her way, his lips pulled to the side as she attempts to entwine her arm through Ben's. My heart thuds once, then returns to its normal pace as I reply 'hi,' taking in her perfection whilst trying not to compare myself to her.

'We should meet up,' says Simon, his attention back on Nat.

'Definitely.' She scours the entrance, left then right, and points at the thick pillar ahead of us, payphones positioned around the edges. Our only connection with the outside world for the next few days. 'How about there? Tomorrow morning. Eleven.'

'Come on boys, I'm hungry,' Bec says, reaching for Ben's hand. He moves it to brush his hair away again and I catch his gaze on me. My cheeks flush and I pull my eyes to the dusty ground.

'Perfect.' Simon raises his hand in a wave, jogging backwards to catch up with Ben and Bec.

Nat grabs me, her eyes wide, and lets out a small squeal.

Saturday

'This. Is. Amazing!' My eyes sweep across the field and fix on the giant stage ahead, a black empty canvas for the headline acts. Enclosed marquees for smaller artists scatter the fenced edges, divided by endless food trucks and bars.

People pitch up across the dry yellow grass. Some cross-legged, others with knees bent as they lean back, their faces raised to the sun. Around the main stage, fans mark their territory, resting against the metal barriers to ensure prime position for today's twelve hours of live music.

'Look, the signing tent.' Natalie runs ahead as Simon grabs the daily festival newspaper. 'Barren Youth will be here. After their set. Please can we come?'

She presses her hands into a prayer position, even though she knows I'll do anything to meet them.

'Have you seen this?' Simon flicks out the paper with a crack. 'It says Prince Charles died.'

'What?' Natalie leans in to read it. 'I don't believe it.'

'Anyway.' Simon slaps the pages together and checks his watch. 'The Variables are on soon.'

'They are so good,' I chip in. 'Rewind had them on their free CD last month.'

'That's where I heard them too.' Ben opens his palm to me with a grin, which I cannot help but return. That smile. It beams from his whole being.

'Let's do it.' Simon dangles his arm casually from Natalie's shoulder as they lead the way, stepping in time together.

Ben and I follow, and I sense he's slowed to keep pace with me. I want to walk faster, but then I'll limp more. I don't want him to see that.

'Is this your first festival?' He looks down at me and one side of his mouth lifts, making my stomach somersault.

'Yeah,' I reply, tucking my hair behind my ear as I rack my brain for something smart to add. 'What about you?'

'We did Glastonbury last year.'

My nerves dissipate as the need to run through my must-see-acts takes over. 'Did you watch Joanie Carson?'

'Yep!' He pops the P and raises his eyebrows at me. 'She was incredible.'

He begins to list every band I pined over during the late-night recordings and my hip jars, making me stumble.

'I got you.' He leans to catch me, cupping my elbow with his hand.

I dip my head so my hair falls over my face, hiding my blushed skin. He holds on for a moment more and I try to find my limp-free walk again.

'You should come with us next year.' He holds the canvas of the Alternative Stage tent door open for me.

'I'd love that.' My heart flips, even though he's probably just being polite.

'Me too.' He smiles at me and our eyes lock. I should look away, but I can't.

'Ben!' The screech of his name slices our gaze in two as Bec flings herself at him, wrapping her arms around his neck. He lifts his hands to loosen her and she drops to the ground. 'I knew I'd find you here, searching for all the new and upcoming bands.'

She plants a loud kiss on his cheek, leaving a bright red lipstick mark like a brand.

'I thought you were with Louise,' Ben says as he rubs at his skin with the flat of his palm.

'Nah.' She wrinkles her nose and slips her hand into his. He pulls it away to free himself.

'I think I'll find Nat.' I turn away, a sense of awkwardness washing over me with each new pursuit she makes to claim him, and peer above the crowd.

'Stay.' Ben reaches towards me.

'Let her go.' Bec waves me off with a flap of her hand as she drapes an arm around him.

Sunday

I stretch my legs to absorb the last of the day's sunshine and the late afternoon breeze ruffles the warm scent of hops mixed with last night's bonfires from my hair. Another flyer rolls past like tumbleweed, and a black and white photocopy of Floyd Jackson stares up at me. A giant

RIP across the top. It catches on the grass, flutters to break free and I grab it.

Dumb Glitter is devastated to announce that Floyd Jackson is dead. In memoriam, Floyd's favourite band from his hometown of Salford will perform tonight's set.

'Anyone sitting here?'

Shading my face with my palm, I look up. A tall figure stands in silhouette above me, brushing the layer of waves from his eyes. Ben.

I shuffle over on the dried flattened grass to offer a seat and his mouth lifts into that half-grin as he crouches next to me.

'Nat said you were here,' he says, and I swallow hard at the thought he wanted to find me. A small line forms between his thick dark eyebrows as his gaze flicks to where my hand is attempting to rub the ache from my leg. 'Are you okay?'

'Me? I'm fine.' I make my smile bigger, and as a distraction I thrust the flyer at him. 'Do you think it's true?'

He shrugs as he takes it. 'He was pretty wild by all accounts.'

'I'll be so gutted if it's real.' I shake my head.

'Sophie?'

My heart leaps to my throat, forgetting the rumour in an instant. It's the first time he's said my name.

'Nat asked—' He hesitates, interrupting himself. 'If I could look after you tonight.'

He found me because Nat said I needed help. She means well, but this isn't something I use to attract people.

117

He folds into a cross-legged position, his hands hanging between his legs. I lift my eyes to his face, filled with concern. I guess there's no point trying to hide it. It's not like I stand a chance anyway, especially with Bec around.

'I have arthritis. In my hip. It's giving me some grief.' I pause to study him. He tilts his head to the side, as if he wants to hear more, and a nervous chuckle rolls from me. 'Not very cool, I know.'

He rotates his arm towards me displaying a long scar above his pink festival band. 'It's not the same, but I have some experience of pain.'

'What happened?'

'I fell from a tree when I was six and it didn't set properly. It twinges sometimes.'

I reach forward, ready to trace the fine line snaking up his skin, and jerk my hand back, my heart pounding.

'And you? Got any good war wounds?'

'Oh yeah.' I grin as I nod. 'I have some pretty impressive ones.'

He shuffles forward on his crossed legs and leans closer.

'Really? Prove it.' He raises one eyebrow.

I press my lips together and glance at the small groups surrounding us on the field.

'I'm not sure it would go down too well if I took my shorts off here to show them.'

'I don't know.' He holds my gaze.

The blush rushes to my cheeks, across my hairline and pops from every follicle. *Did he really just say that?*

'I can't believe they got backstage passes,' I say in a hurry to change the subject. 'Aren't you pissed Simon didn't take you?'

'Nah. I told him to take her. He's liked Nat for ages.' His eyes lift into small crescents. 'How about you?'

I blink fast. *Is he asking if I like anyone?* Then shake my head fast, as if that will offer him some sort of answer.

'What would you like to do for the rest of the day? I'm all yours.' He springs from his sitting position, brushes the dead grass from his jeans, and leans down to me with open palms.

I hesitate for a moment before sliding my hands into his. He wraps each finger around mine, enveloping them within his cool soft skin. Holding just tight enough for me to feel secure, he pulls me upright, our bodies so close I feel the warmth radiating from him. My eyes reach his collarbone and I focus on the divot in the middle, and then my gaze takes in the way his T-shirt moulds to the shape of his chest. My pulse raises, pumping so loud in my ears I'm sure he must hear it.

'Howdy, England!' A deep American voice booms out.

'Is this Ratboy?' My voice breathy as I drag my eyes to the main stage. Ben stretches to see above the gathering audience and nods. 'I didn't realise they were already on.'

'Do you want to see them?' he asks.

I nod and follow him into the crowd as the electric guitar riff to Ratboy's latest song screeches from the speakers.

The chorus kicks in and the singer holds the microphone out to us, his hand cupped around his ear. I glance at Ben, the words bursting from him as he dances.

'They are so good.' Ben shouts across to me.

'I've wanted to see them forever.'

We both turn to the stage as the drums pound.

'I love this one so much.' I raise my hands above my head and clap in time.

'Go on my shoulders.' He scoots down, ready for me to climb up.

'Really?'

'Yes!'

My fingers entwine in the waves of his dark hair as I wrap one leg over, then the other, ignoring the spasm of pain in my joint. His hands grip my thighs as he pushes himself to stand. I hook my feet around his back and the singer howls into the mic, announcing the start of 'Over You.'

'You good?' I look down at him, taking in the freckles scattered above his dark brows.

'I'm great.' He gives me a quick thumbs up, then grabs at my thighs again.

As the song builds Ben and I find our synchronicity, our bodies moving together as the bass pounds through us. I glance behind me at the infinite crowd, coated in the golden light of the setting sun. We bounce in one giant mass as the singer launches into the chorus, his voice cracking with pain every time he repeats, 'he's over you, over you, over you'. Hands stretch skywards, cutting the shadows as the sun dips lower. I raise my arms in a V and belt out the final line with him, with everyone, and it's the most alive I've ever felt.

He bends to his knees, and I climb off, throw my arms around his neck and he lifts me into the air.

'That was the best thing ever,' I say, his soft hair brushing against my cheek.

I pull my head back, my chest pushed into his and my feet inches off the ground. We stare at each other, his eyes darker in the indigo light as his expression turns serious. I bite down on my lip as his chin dips, the corner of his mouth twitching up.

'It's time to see if Floyd Jackson really is dead,' he says, lowering me until the tips of my feet touch the ground. 'Follow me.'

He stretches his hand out and I slide mine in. His fingers wrap around, holding on tight.

We wind through gaps, squeezing past groups and dodging beer spills until we make it to the front. I tilt my head at the stage, looming before us.

He pulls me in front of him, so I'm against the metal barrier. The crowd weave around us in a constant flow, all eager to get closer. Every time someone jostles past, his body presses into me, sending electric bolts through my entire being. He twists his neck to look at me, pumping his thick eyebrows with that beautiful smile, our faces inches apart.

'Hey,' Ben whispers in my ear, as he places his arms either side of me and wraps his hands around the top of the railing as if to create a protective cage. His gaze flicks down to my leg and then back up and I realise how long it's been since I thought about pain. He leans forward, his eyes on fire. I tilt my chin up, lifting myself onto my toes to reach him as a roar rips through the crowd and everyone billows forward, knocking me against the barrier and into the safety of his arm. We stare at each other, paused in the moment, and then grin as the drums start, simple at first, then faster, harder.

'This is it,' he says, and the bass vibrates through my body.

I startle as the twang of a lead guitar screams through the speakers.

Finally, Floyd Jackson's voice bursts through, and he slides onto the stage to join the rest of the band. The crowd erupts and I cup my hands around my mouth to holler.

'Who's here to have a good time?' Floyd Jackson yells out and everyone responds, cheering, screaming, whistling as he stands back and listens, a stupefied grin on his face. 'Who's here to have a *great* time!'

The noise levels rise higher, and the area around us squeezes tight as everyone strains to get closer.

'Well, earlier today I was dead, so I'm here to have a fucken *amazing* time!'

The guitars burst into 'Not Just Anyone', and he leaps around the stage like a released wind-up toy. We all respond, jumping so high it's like we are levitating. Steam lifts, disintegrating into the summer air as the lyrics are roared back at the band. Fists pump with every beat until the last, and all that remains is the vibration of a final electric guitar strum.

I raise my arms to clap, and Ben's hands drop to my waist. He spins me and presses his lips to mine. Soft at first, then harder as my arms lock tight around his neck and my fingers weave into his hair. I push up onto my tiptoes and he raises his palms to the side of my face, holding me as his tongue parts my lips, searching for mine. My body presses itself closer to him as I turn my head, forcing the kiss to get deeper. The next song begins and we are pushed apart in a tidal wave as everyone starts to jump again. He reaches out and tugs me back into his arms, grinning before he whirls me back towards the stage.

For the rest of the set I feel like I'm floating. Ben and I dance together, his arms wrapped around me as though he never wants to be separated. When the band announces the final song, my heart drops, wondering if this means the moment is almost over. I tilt my head to the side with the opening chords and he rests his cheek right next to mine and squeezes me to him.

When the song ends the crowd booms like thunder, whistling and screaming for more. The band bow, throwing out picks and drumsticks and discarded sweaty T-shirts. In another world, I would want these trinkets, but right now all I want is more time with Ben. They ricochet off the stage to another giant explosion before returning to take their final bow.

As the crowd disperses a breeze whips around us, chilling the voids left behind. I lean closer to him as people stumble past, singing, shouting, and laughing as they tell each other their versions of the night. He unwraps his jumper from his waist and pulls it over my head. It drops over me like a dress, passing the tops of my thighs where my shorts end. The sleeves hang off my arms, and he ruffles one side up until he finds my hand and links it with his again.

He leads us across the field out the gates towards the camping grounds. We arrive at his site and creep over guide ropes and past singalongs guided by the soft strums of guitars. His face, bathed in the flickering orange glow of the crackling fires, bends to kiss me again. Trapped within the long sleeves of his jumper I wrap my covered hands around his waist, never wanting to let go.

The zip of his tent rips open and a torch light darts towards us, breaking us apart.

'Bec?' His brows draw into a frown.

'Where have you been?' Bec peers from the tent, a hand clasped around the top of a sleeping bag. Her golden waves tumbling around her bare shoulders. 'I've been waiting for you. Like I said I would.'

I pull away, but his fingers grapple with mine to hold me tighter.

'Wait. Sophie. There's nothing—' He steps forward, but I shake my head remembering how he was only there to look after me. And if he can have her, what would he ever see in me?

'It's okay. I understand.' I raise my palms in surrender and offer a small smile as I turn to make my way through the obstacle course. My name on his lips begging me to come back until I find the path again. I limp towards our tent, stumbling across festival debris, and bury myself within my sleeping bag, shivering despite the warmth of his thick woollen jumper.

Monday

'Sophie, wake up. We have to catch the train.' Nat's eyes light up. 'Wait. Is that Ben's jumper?'

My fingers rise to the neck and run across the soft wool, reliving his hands pulling me close. A sudden weight tugs at my heart, and I turn from the eagerness on her face.

'Did something happen?'

'Nothing happened.' I breathe out hard.

'*Something* happened.'

Her expression changes from wide-eyed excitement to furrowed concern as I confess to our evening together, ending with Bec, naked, in his sleeping bag.

'That sucks,' says Natalie.

My hip aches so much. Without the adrenaline of last night, the pain has doubled. I swallow some tablets and stuff clothes into my backpack.

When we surface, our field is already three-quarters empty. Overflowing rubbish bags and wide divots where guide ropes were tripped over a million times replace the sea of tents. The path is filled with people making their return journey to the real world, still singing and laughing, but with the energy of depleted batteries.

'Do you reckon Prince Charles really *is* dead?' Natalie asks as she rolls the flattened tent across the ground.

'Floyd Jackson wasn't, so I'm pretty sure Charlie's still going strong.'

We pass Ben's campsite and I drop my eyes to my purple boots, their ends tinted with beige dust. My cheeks burn with the embarrassment of getting it all so wrong.

The train pulls in when we arrive at the station and Natalie bags us a table seat. We collapse into the chairs opposite one another as the carriage lines with festival goers finding any free space to crumple into. I lean against the cool glass of the window and close my eyes.

'Anyone sitting here?'

I lift my head to the voice. His voice.

He swallows hard as he waits for my answer, hovering in the aisle as Simon launches himself next to Natalie, wrapping his arm around her.

'You're still wearing my jumper,' Ben says and my cheeks flush.

I lift the bottom to tug it over my head and he raises his hand to stop me.

'Keep it. I like it on you.' He offers me a smile and my heart kicks up a notch. 'Listen. About last night.'

'It's all good.' I flap my hand in front of me like no explanation is needed.

'No. It's not.' He leans towards me. 'Bec is Simon's ex. She's been trying to get with me to make him jealous since they broke up. I swear nothing is going on. With me or with him.'

He nods to the opposite side of the table where his friend is lightly snoring, his head resting against Nat's as she snuggles into the crook of his arm.

'As soon as you left, I made sure she did too,' Ben continues.

'It's okay. It was a fun night, but you don't have to ...' I flick my eyes down.

'It was the best night I've ever had.' He dips his head to try to make me look at him.

I lift my eyes and my stomach flips as they connect with his.

'I came to find you, but when I unzipped your tent, you were asleep.'

'You saw me asleep?' My eyes widen in horror.

'You looked super cute, curled up in your sleeping bag, in my jumper.' He leans closer. 'It took all I had not to climb in there with you.'

I look through the window as we gather speed, trying to hide my grin.

'Can I play you something?' He slides in next to me as he pushes an earbud in, holding the other out for me. I secure it in place, the wire hanging loose between us.

He holds my gaze as he presses 'play' on his Discman. The sharp sound of the opening guitar riff to 'Not Just Anyone' bursts into my ear and Floyd Jackson's voice wails through. He beams at me and I can't help but smile back as his fingers find mine and link them in his. Floyd Jackson is definitely not dead.

SPRUZZI D'AMORE

jenny woolsey

I glanced from the stocktake spreadsheet on my clipboard to the containers sitting on the storeroom shelves. Each container neatly labelled—bandages, syringes, tubes, wipes, tweezers and all manner of sterile medical supplies.

'We need more wound dressings,' I said, my head down as I wrote on the form.

'Um, Mandy?'

A male nurse stood in the doorway dressed in the hospital navy blues and wearing a dazzling smile. A sudden warmth, like my weighted blanket, enveloped me.

'Yes?'

'I'm Roman, Ezrie's replacement. She said to come and see you.'

'Okay. I didn't realise what time it was. If you can do the obs in Room 65 and 66, that would ... would be good.'

'*Piacere di conoscerti.*' He winked, shoved his hands into his pockets and sauntered off.

'What?' I stood, heat in my cheeks, staring out the doorway at the white wall with its *Your health is our priority* poster then closed my mouth and shook my head.

A week later, Ezrie grinned as she sat beside me at the nurse's station and whispered, 'Roman's so cute. He's Italian too. You know what they say about Italian men! Did you see his tight butt?'

'I don't think you should be saying that here,' I whispered back. 'And no, I don't know and I didn't notice.'

In fact, I had noticed he was Italian and cute. That's why I stuttered when we first met but Ezrie didn't need ammunition.

'He's single.' Ezrie showed her pearly white teeth and raised her eyebrows.

I guffawed then took the next patient's folder from the stack. Men were on my 'just friends' list as it had only been three months since I broke off my engagement. My dream of marrying a wealthy handsome man was smashed with my ex-fiancé Corey's final interrogation during my twenty-eighth birthday celebration.

'Where were you this afternoon? You didn't pick up.'

'I was getting groceries. I didn't hear the phone. Sorry.' A knot twisted in my guts and the hairs stood up on my arms.

Corey grabbed my wrist and snapped, 'You *must* answer my calls. I get worried if you don't.' His eyes spat shards of glass.

I yanked my hand back and scowled at him. This was getting beyond a joke and his reactions were way off. In the beginning, his behaviour made me feel special but now it was too much. His constant,

'I get worried if you don't pick up … why weren't you home at 6:00 pm … you must tell me what you're doing,' was suffocating and wearing. Ezrie's previously unwanted advice, given on multiple occasions, burned like a soldering iron in my thoughts. 'Love is not controlling. Love is not knowing your every move. Love is trust and respect. He isn't treating you right. You deserve so much better. You need to get out.'

After pulling my hand back, I shuddered, my skin sizzled and I tore off the three-carat diamond ring, flinging it across the table. I'd finally had enough. Ezrie was right.

'I deserve more!' I snapped. 'I'm not a possession like your Lamborghini. You don't have to know everything I'm doing … I don't want to marry you anymore.'

He put his hand to his face as though he'd been slapped.

'Baby, come on,' he said. 'You don't mean that. Let's talk about this.'

I grabbed my coat and handbag and rushed from the restaurant, sobs wracking my body.

Ezrie nudged my ribs and pointed. I parked my thoughts and studied Roman. He was leaning on an overbed table filling out a form. He stopped writing to speak to a patient wearing a moon-boot. The elderly lady patted him on the arm and smiled broadly. In addition to the obvious attractions, he was caring.

'You're staring,' Ezrie teased.

'Am not,' I said. 'I'm not interested in another relationship. You know that.'

She patted my shoulder. 'I'll do my rounds.'

131

What I'd said to Ezrie was true. Roman was lovely, and probably a real catch, but once bitten twice shy as they say. And twice bitten in my books equated to becoming a born-again virgin. Tyler, my first, and then Corey were the type of men I thought I wanted. Wealthy, protective and loving the fast life. But both became more and more controlling once the love bombing wore off and I became more and more of a possession. If I'd made this mistake in choosing these types of men twice, would I do it again? I couldn't chance that. It was safer to stay single.

A month passed. Roman had become a regular on the ward and at times I caught myself staring at him. His gentle and friendly nature floated around like fluffy white clouds.

'Mandy?'

I lifted my head from my paperwork. Roman's fresh cologne, with its hint of citrus, massaged my senses.

'Does Marjorie need something again?'

'Er, no, she's fine. Her son's with her.' A tendril of hair fell across his left eye and he looked like a little lost boy. I had the sudden urge to reach out and push it back behind his ear.

'I have a spare ticket to see *Moulin Rouge* at QPAC and I was wondering if you'd like to come with me?'

'Ah, um,' I stammered. 'Ah ... no, I don't think so.'

'Oh,' Roman said, his smile fading. 'Well, would you like to go to the movies or something?'

My mouth opened to decline again but I closed it. *Oh, he was so lovely ... and one date couldn't hurt. It didn't even have to be a date. But ... I couldn't ... I didn't ... I mustn't ...*

His crystal blue eyes drew me into their sparkling depths and I couldn't resist.

'Actually, *Moulin Rouge* sounds amazing. When?'

Roman grinned. 'Tonight! See you at seven.' He turned away and walked off.

I covered my face with my hands. What had I done?

'Roman,' I called, but he didn't respond.

Mrs Birmingham's bell rang and, as I headed to Bed 43, I rationalised that *Moulin Rouge* wasn't going to be a date. It was just a night out to the theatre with a new friend. Nothing else.

The thick maroon curtains closed on the Lyric Theatre stage, signalling the end of the *Moulin Rouge* production. During the finale, rapturous applause filled the theatre like water in an aquarium.

Throughout the performance I sat spellbound by the dancing, the music, the sets and the songs. 'That was amazing!' I squealed like a little girl gifted a bag of fairy floss.

Roman smiled. 'I thought you'd like it. Would you like to get something to eat?'

'Sure.' I pulled my faux-fur wrap around my shoulders.

'I know a quaint little place overlooking the river,' Roman said as we walked up the Southbank boulevard.

'It's beautiful here with all the lights,' I said. I loved Brisbane at night. It was magical. I could imagine the fairies living in each tree and painting the little twinkling stars everywhere while people slept.

'So, what is your favourite thing to do apart from work?' Roman asked, sticking his hands in his pockets.

'I like to read memoirs and grow succulents.'

'You're kidding me!' Roman exclaimed. 'I have a garden full of succulents.'

'Really?' I'd never met a man interested in growing succulents and we discussed propagation methods all the way to the restaurant and through dinner. He knew so much.

At the night's end, a happiness I'd never felt before coursed through me. Roman was even nicer than I thought and he was obsessed with succulents!

Ding.

I stared at my phone's screen. This was the twentieth message Corey had sent me in the past six weeks.

It read: *I am so sorry Mandy. I love you. Come back to me.*

I initially replied to his messages but Ezrie told me to stop and block them. I hadn't blocked them but I wasn't responding to them anymore.

'You should take out a Domestic Violence Order against him. He's stalking you,' Ezrie said matter-of-factly one night. Upon leaving the hospital, Corey had suddenly appeared from the side of the building and pleaded, 'I'm really, really, really sorry, Babe. Please, I need you in my life. I won't ask you where you are anymore.'

In shock, I turned and walked straight back in through the hospital doors, seeking safety in a clinic's examination room. The receptionist called security who hustled him on.

I scrolled through the messages, all of a similar nature. *Loves me, wants me back, can't live without me.* A shiver coursed from my head to my toes as a vision flashed before me of last night's news reporting a beautiful lady killed by her ex-partner. This was getting too far out of control ... He had to stop. Maybe it was time to take out a DVO.

The time on the fob watch, pinned to my uniform, was 4:45 pm. The watch had been Grandma's, then Mum's. I was proudly the third generation of nurses in my family. My forebears had immersed themselves in paediatrics whereas I enjoyed orthopaedics. Bones, like succulents, fascinated me.

I completed my handover to Peter then collected my lunchbox and handbag.

'Have a good night.'

'You too.'

'I'm off home to talk to my succulents.'

Peter raised an eyebrow at me.

Roman had invited me out tonight to see a movie but I declined, feigning a desire for a night at home. I wanted to go out with him but this stuff with Corey was scaring me off. It was safer to say no.

On my balcony, the multitude of portulacas spilt over their pots. 'You're growing so well!' I told them as the water droplets glistened on their leaves.

I went inside, opened the freezer, took out a microwave mac'n'cheese, pressed five minutes and watched the numbers count backwards as the meal went around and around.

My mind turned to Roman. Maybe I should have said yes to the movie. It would have been fun. Maybe I should let my guard down with him. Unless he was faking it, he wasn't anything like Tyler or Corey ... and he was sweet.

'I'm off to the library. Do you want to come?' Roman asked me the next day at work as I strolled to the lift with my lunchbox and book. I liked to spend my breaks sitting outside on the blue bench under the big leafy tree and read. I did this each shift.

He pulled two library barcoded novels out of his backpack.

I did have a book to return. 'Um, ah ... okay.'

'I thought by your long pause you were going to say no again!' His face lit up like a sparkler on Christmas Eve.

I smiled.

Books of all different sizes with spines of different colours and fonts filled shelves. I loved the quietness of the library and the excitement of finding another interesting memoir to read.

I laughed as Roman pulled books off shelves and, using quirky accents, quoted a line from them. I didn't know if he was right or just being silly.

I held the two books I was going to borrow. One was Michelle Obama's memoir and the other was Prince Harry's. I glanced at my watch. It was time to go.

Roman came up beside me and handed me a book. I read the cover, 'I Think You're Sexy.'

'That's an interesting title. I've got Prince Harry's memoir.' I showed him the book with the red-head's portrait on the front.

Roman touched my arm, winked and said, 'I think you're sexy.'

My mouth gaped open like a goldfish and I blushed. 'Thank you!'

'Am I sexy?' he asked me, winking at me again.

'Um, yes, you are,' I said, feeling hot and awkward.

Voices filled the ward. It was handover time. I told Margaret, the next nurse, about my patients and headed for the lift. I was looking forward to checking on my succulents, particularly the Hens and Chicks I was trying to propagate. Then I would bathe in relaxation salts. I planned on spending the night with Prince Harry while lying on the couch under my blankie.

Floor 4, 3, 2, 1. I exited the lift and headed for the hospital's entrance doors. They opened to reveal a sky radiating a warm glow of orange and yellow with splashes of pink. It was a glorious sunset. The sun, beginning to kiss the horizon, was harsh on my eyes and I stopped to grab my sunglasses from my handbag.

Whack!

A flash and excruciating pain to my chin sent me reeling backwards. My mind tried to make sense of what was happening. Who was attacking me? I stared up into the face. It was Corey.

He swung again at me but missed when I stumbled.

My vision blurred as the shock smashed me.

'You're mine, Mandy,' he said.

'What are you doing?' I spluttered.

Yells of 'Stop it!' and 'Leave her alone!' filled the air. Someone shouted, 'Get down on the ground!'

'I just wanted to talk to the bitch,' Corey yelled.

I glimpsed the glint of a knife.

'Get down on the ground, now!' yelled a police officer.

'Oh, my god!' I screamed.

Corey resisted and lunged at him. A taser sent Corey to the pavement.

137

'Mandy, we'll get you inside.' Brett, one of the orthopaedic doctors, gently placed his hand on my arm. I nodded, the pain in my chin and jaw growing.

'Mandy, are you okay?'

Roman stood in front of me and I shook my head then fell forwards, crumpling into his arms.

My jaw ached, so I must be alive.

I slowly opened my eyes, groaned, and perused the familiar setting. The blue curtains on the rail, the board with my name and the name of the nurse who was caring for me ... I had swapped places with one of my patients.

'Hey, you're awake.'

I looked at Roman who sat on a chair beside me. He stood up and gently hugged me.

'Did Corey punch me?'

'I believe so,' Roman answered. 'Ezrie said he did.'

I squeezed my eyes shut then reopened them as I tried to push away an invasion of ugly thoughts. Roman's warm hand found my cold one.

An x-ray showed I didn't have a fractured jaw and I was able to go home the next morning.

'I'm glad the police slapped a DVO on the mongrel,' Roman said to me three days later as we sat together on the blue bench eating lunch. The shiner on my jaw glowed.

'Ezrie said I should have done it earlier. I was going to but I didn't think he would attack me.'

Roman put his arm around my back. 'From now on, I'll protect you. Who's your favourite superhero?'

'Lois Lane. Some people don't think she is a superhero but they're wrong.'

'Well, I'll be your Clark Kent—your Superman.' Roman winked at me.

'But they are ...' I said trailing off, my heart perfecting a backflip.

'We could be too,' Roman said. 'Would you be my girlfriend?'

I faltered for a minute as a debating team took over my mind. *It's too soon. You must say no because you don't need a boyfriend ... But it isn't too soon. You know enough about him. You know he isn't like Corey.*

I smiled. The winner of the debate spoke, 'Clark Kent, I would love to be your girlfriend.'

'*Grazie.*' Roman bent over and kissed my lips until I quivered.

'It's too soon to be in a relationship,' my mother said to me when I rang home to share my happy news.

'I know, Mum, but he's so nice. I'm not making the same mistake.'

'Why don't you remain friends for a while? I thought you were going to have time being single. That's what you told me.'

'Mum, I like him.'

'Well, liking him is fine. You don't have to be in a relationship. It's too soon. I'm unimpressed, Amanda. You need to really think carefully about this. Your father's not happy, either.'

Dad got on the phone. 'Listen to your mother.'

Upon hanging up, depression dumped itself on my shoulders. How could I be Roman's girlfriend if they disapproved? I was an adult and should do as I please but my parents meant the world to me. I didn't want there to be tension over this.

I couldn't ...

The clouds were black, threatening rain. They matched my mood. I had to tell Roman today we were breaking up. As it started to spit, tears filled my eyes. I wiped them away.

'Morning, sweetheart,' Roman said as he greeted me in the ward. 'What's wrong?'

I was going to wait until morning tea but instead I blurted out, 'I have to break up with you. I can't do this.'

Roman stared at me, his face turning white.

'I'm sorry but I need to do my handover.' I rushed past him.

For the rest of my shift, I stayed as far away from Roman as I could. When my shift was over, I asked Peter if Roman had gone home. He had.

That night, I checked on my succulents. My babies were sprouting. I was happy with my Chain of Turtles. I should have been ecstatic but instead I felt miserable.

I heated up another mac'n'cheese and lay on the couch with Harry and my blankie.

After rereading a page five times, I gave up and turned on the TV.

I flicked from one station to the next to the next to the next.

I switched the TV off and threw down the remote.

I lay staring up at the lightbulb above me until I drifted off from mental exhaustion.

For two weeks I avoided Roman by changing my shifts so we weren't on at the same time. It was tricky at handover time but we were never in the same rooms.

Ezrie noticed my low mood. 'Why are you listening to your parents?'

'Because they've always had my back and I don't want bad blood between us.'

'But he's not like Corey at all.'

'Yeah, I know …'

After each shift, I slunk home. I talked to my Liveforever succulents, read my memoirs and lay on the couch wrapped in my blankie.

Sadness became my boyfriend.

'Cheer up!' Mum told me. 'You're being a misery guts.'

'I can't,' I flatly told her. 'I really like Roman and if you got to know him, I think you would too.'

Ezrie stared at me over the nurse station's desk. I averted my eyes.

'I'm going to take you out tonight,' she said. 'You've been hibernating long enough.'

I shook my head.

'I'm not going to take no for an answer.'

I sighed. 'Where are we going?'

'It's a surprise!' she said, winking at me.

I furrowed my eyebrows. 'I don't like surprises, you know that.'

'You'll like this. Wear something nice.'

I stared at the clothes in my cupboard. Most were shades of blue, purple or black.

Wear something nice.

I pulled out my favourite mid-blue top and a pair of white pants, blue being my favourite colour as it matched my eyes.

I touched up my make-up and slipped on a pair of ankle boots.

Knock, knock.

I opened the door.

'Ready?' Ezrie looked me up and down. 'Pretty.'

'Where are we going?' I buckled up in Ezrie's little car and she zipped in and out of the traffic.

'It's a surprise.'

'But you know I hate surprises.'

Ezrie grinned and turned the music up.

We stopped in Fortitude Valley under the Story Bridge.

'We're here,' Ezrie said. 'Come with me.'

We walked over to the fence. The Brisbane River's dark ripples lapped against the rocks and the little blue lights sparkled like sequins on the steel beams of the bridge.

'Turn around.' Ezrie grabbed my hand and spun me.

'Oh.' Standing there, dressed in a navy suit with Strings of Pearls succulents clipped to his hair, was Roman. A cloth hung over his arm.

'Benvenuta bella signora,' he said with a smile.

Ezrie appeared with folding chairs and a table. She set them up, spread a blue tablecloth and placed a wicker picnic basket and a bucket with a bottle of wine on top.

'I'm off now,' she said with a grin. 'Have a good night, Mandy and Roman.'

I stared from Ezrie to Roman.

This is a set up!

Familiar music filled the air. *Moulin Rouge.*

'May I have this dance?' Roman asked me, flinging the cloth towards the table.

'Only if you take the pearls off your head.' I laughed.

He chuckled. 'You don't like my new hairdo?'

He bent over so I could unclip them. I laid the Strings of Pearls on the table and melted into his outstretched arms.

I smelt his cologne and his masculinity. I snuggled into his chest. It felt safe. It felt secure. It felt right …

The rest of the evening we feasted on chicken, salad and bread rolls followed by crème caramel and strawberries for dessert.

I drank too much wine, splashing it on my top and I didn't care. I giggled at Roman's anecdotes of his university job as a pizza delivery driver until my face and belly hurt.

Roman took my hand and we walked over to the fence to look at the river. Small boats with lights flashing motored by and the City Cats cruised back and forth, creating ripples. A playful dolphin surfaced and splashed water onto the nearby jetty.

'Mandy?'

'Mmmm?'

'I've really missed you. Maybe I can come and spend time with your parents so they see I'm not like your exes. Ezrie said that's why you broke up with me.'

'It is, but I'm also scared of making a mistake again.'

'Do you think I'm a mistake?'

The lights from the bridge lit up Roman's face. His eyes were moist. My heart hammered.

'No.'

'So, let's take the chance.' Roman's soft sensual lips met mine as our bodies melted together.

The embers floating in the air from the log fire were mesmerising. The cabin was toasty warm, the carbonara delicious and filling and the fruity wine was making me a little light-headed.

Roman and I were in Stanthorpe enjoying a Christmas in July weekend.

True to his word, Roman visited Mum and Dad. They had interrogated him and been suspicious of his intentions but it didn't take long for their initial concerns to vanish.

'I really like him,' Mum told me on one of our phone calls, 'and your father does too.'

'Good,' I said. 'I told you he wasn't like the other two.'

'He's a good man,' Mum said. 'He'll make a good son-in-law.'

'Hang on, Mum,' I replied with a smile. 'Let's not get too hasty.'

To the refrains of, *I Will Love You Forever*, Roman pulled me close and stroked my hair. I closed my eyes. 'Mandy, I'm falling in love with you. In fact, *ti amo*,' he whispered.

I opened my eyes and turned towards him. 'I'm falling in love with you too.'

As our lips tenderly touched, a warmth flooded my body just as it had the first time we'd met back in the storeroom and I quivered. '*Infatti, ti amo molto.*'

Roman pulled back to look at me. 'You're learning Italian?'

I kissed his lips. '*Sì, tesoro mio.*'

THE BOY WITH KALEIDOSCOPE EYES

lily mulholland

Lucy Diamond, named after The Beatles' song, had never had a boyfriend.

Not by choice, but by circumstance. It began when her date—Sean Coley, the boy she'd been sweet on for two years—hadn't arrived to collect her for her year-twelve formal. He'd decided to go with Helen Swain instead and hadn't bothered to tell her. Lucy had sat on the sofa in her front room, first with nervous anticipation, and later with tears that etched new patterns into her watermarked taffeta dress, until her mother had forced her to go to bed.

The following week, the last of the year, the small-town girls at school had tittered behind her back while the boys laughed in her face. She'd tried to beg off from going to class but the farm-hardened school nurse was having none of it. Recess and lunch were spent in the toilets hiding, crying. By the end of the week, she had been in such a state her English teacher thought Lucy was having a heart attack and called 000. Cruel taunts followed her as the paramedics loaded her into the ambulance and took her off to hospital.

When Lucy couldn't get out of bed her mother looked after her, arranging for the doctor to house visit. She borrowed books from the library in those first few months, then bought new clothes as Lucy needed them, and cut her hair. As one year became many, her mother cocooned her from a cruel world. Lucy was twenty-nine and didn't need to go out, and she didn't until ... her mother died suddenly. Lucy was alone for the first time in her life. Moving past her front door was unthinkable. Facing the outside world was inconceivable. And yet. She wasn't ready to forgo all human connection. Lucy waded through her options and took control of her life. First came a new computer and modem financed by her small inheritance. Then, from the safety of her sofa, she learnt to browse the world's online catalogues that delivered to her doorstep. From online directories, she organised the removal of her garbage and a gardener to tend to the cottage garden. With the world at her fingertips, Lucy completed her final year of school, did a degree online, and set up a successful boutique marketing company with a staff of three. She had all the money she needed to live a comfortable and happy life inside her childhood home. While she adored her workmates, there was no intimacy; no one knew her well enough to coax her deep desires out into the light.

She flicked open her calendar app, ready to start the weekly three o'clock team catch-up. She poured herself a cheeky white wine and grabbed the hummus and carrot sticks from the fridge. Sumudu, Cameron, and Abigail were her friends as well as her employees and she encouraged them to bring a drink to the meeting, a virtual cocktail hour.

Just as the meeting connected, a *click* and *zhmm* cut through the background drone of the air conditioning. The cool air stilled, the lights went out and her notebook screen dimmed, fading to black the three smiling faces waiting expectantly. *Bugger!* A quick text let them know she'd tripped a switch and would be straight back. Phone in pocket, Lucy did what her therapist recommended: put her big-girl pants on and go to the front door.

A violent chill shook her, and she took a moment to breathe. The power box was on the outside of the house, and, though she hated to step through the front door, if she kept one hand on the house—the weatherboards a talisman to her touch—she could just about summon sufficient courage to reach it.

She edged across the verandah, grateful it wrapped around the side of the house. Above the cut grass scent of the town's wide nature strips, the perfume of her mother's climbing Westerland roses reached her, giving her the courage to step forward. Her reward was the old green power box. She flipped the covering open, discovering all circuit breakers had tripped. *Damn!*

Back safely inside, she took some steadying breaths before bringing up the power company's website on her phone. No unscheduled interruptions. She rang them. All looked good on their end, must be a customer-end issue.

She could not afford to be offline. Her phone battery would only last a few more hours and then all her lifelines to the outside world would be gone. A text to her team deferred their meeting, while she scrambled to find an electrician. She posted an urgent notice to the community Facebook group using her online moniker Lou Sea, requesting recommendations for a reliable electrician with excellent customer service. The last thing she wanted was a burly man trudging through her house, answering her questions with monosyllables and filling its rooms with his foetid aromas.

By the time she finished her glass of wine, schooling herself to sip not gulp, she had five recommendations against her post. One included a weblink, so she clicked on it and checked out Lightgood Leckies. What on earth was a Leckie? Or was it Lecky? No idea. But she did appreciate a fine example of nominative determinism.

'Hello? I have a power outage at my house and the energy company tells me it's at my end. I run my business from home so I was hoping you could come today?' she asked as she straightened the wine coaster. It was presumptuous to ask for a same-day call-out this late in the afternoon, but she was in a pickle.

'You can? Really? I'm so grateful.' Relief flooded her. 'What? Ah, of course. It's twenty-three Bugden Avenue.' There was a pause at the other end. 'That's right. Oh, sorry. Yes, Lucy Diamond.' The voice on the other end turned gruff. She kept hers light and polite. 'Well, thank you. I will see you at four-thirty.'

Lucy stared at the phone on the table as though it were a scrying mirror. What could she have said to upset the man? A ten-plus year absence from people meant she didn't have every social cue down pat, but surely that was the most innocuous conversation she'd had all year.

She checked the time. Ten to three—ninety minutes to get the house shipshape. Not that it was dirty or messy. She had her routines, and first impressions mattered, especially when she admitted so few visitors. After throwing all the windows open hoping for a breeze, dusting every horizontal surface, straightening anything that could be, and moving magazines from one spot to another, Lucy checked her reflection in the bathroom mirror. She rarely wore make-up—only when she had to present (virtually) at a conference. Would a lick of mascara help the colour of her eyes pop? In this heat it would probably melt off her eyelashes, turning her into a racoon. She surveyed her figure. Not too bad for a woman on the wrong side of thirty. Her clothes weren't exactly fashionable (there were two blazers in the cupboard she wore for client Zoom meetings, but the rest of the week she devoted to jersey tops and Ponte pants). She tucked her hair behind diamond-studded ears. Hair across her face could inadvertently make her appear more attractive. Did she want that kind of attention from the electrician? The last man in the house had been the undertaker. *Had it really been that long?*

She straightened the hand towel and made one more pass through the house, where she realigned the sofa cushions, made sure the blinds were even, and the framed photographs were level.

Moments later, a rhythmic knock at the front door made her heart echo its beat. She smoothed her hair in the hallway mirror, took a deep breath in, two three, out, two three, and peeled open the front door.

Before her stood a man.

A man with pants sitting on hips below a trim waist and some miraculous T-shirt fabric that accentuated his broad shoulders and every other muscle.

A man with ginger hair and a close-clipped beard and moustache with dashing touches of blond.

A man with hazel eyes so magnetic they threatened to pull her in.

'Hello, Lucy.'

Lucy couldn't move. Well, her brain's synapses were whizzing like fast skis over snow, but her traitorous body—Would. Not. Budge.

Who was this man and how did he know her? Because know her he did—the tone of his voice and the look that enthralled her said they were not strangers. She rifled her memories but came up empty.

Come on, Lucy. Let him in.

Nope, she couldn't move. One hand stuck fast to the door frame. Her feet planted hip width apart remained rooted to the timber beneath. The only things working were her heart and lungs. And her overthinking brain, of course.

Come on, Lucy, say something. Anything.

'What's a Leckie?'

Okay, not that.

The man blinked once, cocked his head, and threw it back as a belly laugh erupted, revealing a smile to rival Luna Park's.

Wait. While his laughter was infectious, hadn't people lost the plot since the pandemic? So, she'd asked something embarrassing. The heat in her face told her that. But was he laughing at her? If he was, she should absolutely, positively, send him on his way. There'd been enough laughing at her expense to fill a lifetime.

Before she could coax her body into action, he wiped his eyes with his spare hand, composed himself, and gestured to the toolbox he carried in the other.

'May I come in, Lucy?'

His rich voice unlocked something inside her and calmed the wild imaginings of her brain. She stepped aside, allowing him to pass, and closed the door as his confident gait led her straight down the hall to the kitchen.

'Can I put this on the table?'

At her nod, he carefully deposited the toolbox on the oak kitchen table that had been her grandmother's. He ran his fingers across the varnished top. A pianist, testing a new instrument.

He moved over to her grandmother's gas cooker, the pride of her kitchen, its teal enamel in pristine condition.

'I see you kept it.'

Freeze-frame.

This man had been in her house before? She took another look at his face. Obscured by the facial hair, she had little hope of placing him.

What was his name again? She assessed it against long-boxed memories. Lightgood. Lightgood. Lightgood. Good lord!

'*Gordon Lightgood?*'

His eyes crinkled. 'Ah, the lady remembers me.'

The air sucked from her body; her past had finally found her. Nausea washed through her like dye into muslin. The room went yellow as she fell.

She awoke on the sofa in the living room, the ceiling fan above her still when it should be whirling. That's right, the power had gone out. What was the time? She remembered her crazy dream about Gordon Lightgood.

As Lucy looked for her phone, she heard whistling from her bedroom.

What? She hadn't dreamt Gordon Lightgood. He was really here.

She padded quietly down the hall to her room, peered around the doorframe. Yep, there he was, running some kind of gadget over the wall. He made a note in a notebook and turned, his face instantly shifting from business to pleasure.

'The patient awakes.'

'What happened?'

'You fainted and I caught you. I carried you to the couch, thought it would be more comfortable than the slate in your kitchen.'

Gordon Lightgood's hands had been on her? Touching her body? Lucy's stomach flipped.

'I guess I should thank you.'

Gordon Lightgood was in her bedroom, and she was thanking him? And was she ever going to stop saying his full name in her head?

'You probably should thank me for that, because you are not going to when I tell you how much it's going to cost to repair your electrics.'

The way he looked at her left her stomach aflutter. His charisma was new. Well, since she'd last seen him ... last decade? This was ridiculous. She was a fully-grown woman, with a rebellious body acting out as though she was still seventeen, unable to resist a boy who paid her the slightest attention. Especially one with tourmaline eyes. How had she not noticed all those years ago?

Get a grip, Lucy.

Another breath in ... and out.

Mischief danced in his eyes and were those *dimples* under the well-kept beard?

How was this Gordon Lightgood? Granted, she struggled to remember anything specific, anything remarkable about him. He had been mates with Sean, sure, but he'd just been a freckly, enthusiastic redhead she'd been friendly with. Back then she'd only had eyes for Sean. If she looked hard enough, seventeen-year-old Gordon was almost visible beneath the facial hair. But looking at him was dangerous. Made her want to trace her fingertips along his jawline, have the prickles on his chin transmit his desire into her body.

Cut it out!

Tea. Yes, they should have—

'Tea!' First, she had fainted and now she was screeching.

Oh my god, woman.

The heat rose in her cheeks again and other parts of her body she hadn't thought about in a long time.

His verdelite eyes didn't leave her as he slipped the notebook and device into his leg pocket, a smile playing at the corners of his mouth. 'A cup of tea would be perfect.'

Sending up a prayer of gratitude for his chivalry, she led the way to the kitchen, where he pulled out a chair for her and bade her to sit while he busied himself with the stove and kettle. He certainly knew his way around the kitchen. A tantalisingly attractive quality in a man.

He sat opposite and slid a mug her way. 'Good or bad news first?'

That voice of his was doing things to her insides she could not (and, let's be honest, did not want to) control. Lucy sipped at her tea, letting the vanilla scent calm her racing pulse and thoughts.

Clearing her throat, she put on her serious face. 'Bad.'

He mirrored her change, the cheeky look replaced by a more appropriate business demeanour. 'Okay, so, the wiring in this place is at least one hundred and twenty years old. Possibly more. It's kaput. I'll need to replace a lot of it. Not all. There are some areas that are still conducting well, but the rest of it is tenuous. The outage was caused by a short-circuit inside your dining room wall.' At her confused look, he added, 'It's the main conduit from your power box into the house.'

'What am I looking at in terms of dollars?'

'I can't give you an exact price until I've done some more investigation, but rough ballpark, fifteen to twenty thousand. Could be worse than I think it is. Could be better.'

Lucy did her best not to choke on the tea she was trying to swallow. She had the money—it wasn't like she was saving for a holiday—but she had been planning to redecorate, spruce the place up a little.

'God, you'd better tell me the good news.'

A full smile curved his lips, revealing shiny teeth ... and she had the sudden urge to run her tongue ...

Whoa, whoa, whoa. What the hell, brain?

'I've found the busted wire. If you let me cut into your wall, I can put in a temporary fix, and get your power back on in an hour. If you agree to me doing the rest of the work, I won't charge you for it.' He winked at her.

A little laugh escaped her lips—he was punning with her. She returned fire. 'Based on the current information, I believe I have little choice other than to engage you.'

He held out his hand and shook hers once it was enclosed in his. She could swear she felt a little spark between their fingers but couldn't tell whether it was real or the thrill of new puns—of which she was both collector and connoisseur.

'I'll be done by dinner, but I can't start the other work until next Wednesday.'

'Will the fix last till then?'

'I've learnt to do things right the first time, Ms Lucy Diamond.'

It wasn't until he squeezed her hand that she realised she hadn't released his.

'...and the project should be finished by the end of this week. I'll get the client to ... Lucy, who is that?' asked Cameron from beyond the screen.

She didn't need to turn to know Gordon was behind her, his presence tangible. He'd been working on her wiring for a week. Having him in the house no longer spooked her. In fact, if she was honest, she looked forward to his arrival each day.

Right now, he was currently ripping out old cabling from the living room, her digital office powered by a battery he'd set up for her, to keep the lights on, so to speak, while the rest of them were out.

'The electrician, remember I told you the whole place needs rewiring?' Was Cameron salivating? His lips had gone a funny shape.

'Uh, you did. What you failed to mention is how smoking hot he is. Tell him he can rewire me anytime.'

'Cameron Prentice, you are a very naughty boy.'

'And that's why you all love me and let me join your girl gang.'

'It's a good thing for us that you are safely tucked up in Adelaide,' Sumudu said, killing herself laughing through the monitor.

Gordon coughed loudly. 'I can hear you.'

'Okay, everyone, focus. Abigail, any issues with the Marsden account?'

'No, it's all in hand. I'll call you if anything changes, but I'm on target to close the campaign ahead of schedule.'

'Anything else?'

'Yes.' Sumudu giggled. 'Mr Electrician, a moment?'

Lucy was going to kill them.

'You rang?' Gordon's voice sounded next to her ear, sending shivers down her back as he leant over her shoulder to get his face into the webcam picture.

'Lucy is very important to us, so I just want to make sure you do a very thorough job for her, okay?'

Did they have no shame? She was ready to die of embarrassment.

'I fully intend to.' The deep tones lacing his voice with intent sent heat down below her stomach.

She was definitely going to kill them. 'Okay, you lot. Back to work. See you next week.'

Ending the meeting, she went to push her chair back, but Gordon was still behind her.

'It was nice to meet your friends.' His hands landed gently on her shoulders. 'Lucy, I have to tell you something.'

The light tone had turned heavy, thick, which she recognised as his serious voice. She slipped out from beneath his hands. 'Wait here. I'll be back with wine.'

Returning with two glasses, she found him settled on the sofa, his tools packed away. She handed him a glass and sat opposite.

'Spill it. Not the wine. Whatever it is that is making you nervous.'

His unease was making her anxious. She sipped at her wine. Anything to avoid whatever mortification was coming next.

'Leckie is short for electrician.'

She groaned. Now he'd said it, it was obvious. Wait, was he avoiding the subject too, now that they were face-to-face, eye-to-hope-filled-eye?

'Thanks for the explainer. But that isn't what you wanted to tell me, is it?'

As he lifted his glass to his lips, his hand trembled. He chanced a sip. 'I just wanted to tell you how sorry I am about everything that happened.'

The stricken look on his face told her he wasn't talking about her wiring.

'I want you to know that I hated Sean for what he did. When he turned up at the formal with Helen, I lost my shit. He was supposed to be there with you. And I was waiting to see you. I wanted to ...' He gulped at his wine.

'Wanted to what? Defend my honour? No one was there for me.' The residual anger still made her cheeks burn.

As his eyes lifted slowly from the bottom of his glass, the green mingled with brown, sparkled with golden light.

Now she remembered.

He was the one who had always picked her for his team in PE. The one who'd offered to partner with her for their science pracs. The one who'd helped her carry home her French diorama. She'd only had eyes for Sean, while Gordon had been with her ... for her ... and the whole time, she'd been blind to it.

Her voice soft, 'Wanted to what, Gordon?'

'Ask you to dance. And tell you that I ...'

As he pressed his lips together, she felt his pain. She had hurt him too.

158

'Dammit! Sean ruined everything. The week after the formal, I tried to speak to you at school, but you were either in class or in the girls' toilets. I tried to visit you here too, but your mum sent me away. Said he had damaged you beyond repair.'

Lucy put her wine down on the side table. Took Gordon's and put it next to hers. She wrapped her hands around his. Definite sparks.

'No, he didn't. He was a dick, absolutely, but I was the one who had the breakdown. I wasn't ready for those big feelings, and I couldn't cope.'

Her heart rate spiked as his kaleidoscope eyes relayed an unmistakable signal.

'And now?' His voice, low and hoarse, triggered an electrical surge.

She felt its power.

She was power.

While not yet ready to embrace the world, Gordon, the salve for her wounds, had already begun to help her heal.

She reached up and placed her hands on his cheeks, pulled his face towards her and joined the charged kiss that would change everything.

TAHITIAN JEWEL

elizabeth spratt

No one watching her. She was safe. Aislin perched on the resort's pier, swung her legs back and forth, the tips of her toes splashing turquoise water. A smile burst across her face. She flicked a tangle of curls that danced in front of her eyes. Tranquil. That was the word she was searching for since she'd arrive days ago. It was more than a search for the right word, it was what she wanted to feel in her life. Freedom to be herself.

A motor hummed in the distance, and she twisted her head to the left, the water a flat crystal blue.

It was a small boat. Thank goodness. There wouldn't be a large group of people to interact with. She'd already broken her vow of staying in solitude in her overwater bungalow. The temptation to swim with whales in Tahiti, too strong a drawcard.

She swung her legs back onto the pier, pushed herself up and straightened her hibiscus sarong.

A rugged man tanned and sporting green board shorts and a five o'clock shadow tossed a rope round the black mooring pole. He leapt from the boat and tightened the rope.

She gasped and instantly wanted to kick herself. *No men.* She stole a second look—oops too long. But he oozed sexiness and she felt foolish. She admonished herself, she wasn't some lovesick teen. For crying out loud, she was twenty-seven. But her heart pounded at a frantic pace. *He's probably married. Stop it. No men.* But she could still look.

He pushed his sunglasses onto the top of his short brown hair. 'Olivier. And you must be Ais ...'

His blue eyes pierced right through her. She melted quicker than an ice-cream. That look, she knew that look. She cleared her throat and shuffled her straw bag from one hand to the other before stuttering, 'Hot. The weather. I mean the weather.'

He smiled.

Her hand swiped at her face. *Pull it together girl and introduce yourself.* 'Aislin MacDonagh. It's not pronounced how it's written. It's like ASH-lyen. It means dream.' She wanted to smack herself. Stop pratting. His French accent was to blame, it just elevated his sexiness.

He grinned.

Dimples. Was there anything this guy didn't have?

'Welcome ASH-lyen.'

He was laughing at her. She rubbed one foot against the other. 'And it is just yourself today.'

Not a question. A blunt summary. Today, tomorrow, and forever it would just be her. 'Yes.'

'Perfect.'

Could those dimples get even bigger and cuter? *Stop it Aislin. No men!*

'Let me help you on board. We are just waiting for two more people.'

Aislin gripped his extended hand. She couldn't describe the sensation that flooded her body. No wedding rings. *Remember no men, you are content with being the fun-loving aunt.* But there was the telltale flutter.

'Sit anywhere, the skipper is Joe.'

'Morning Joe.' Her gaze still on Olivier.

'Ah, Aislin, you can let go of my hand now.'

Heat exploded across her cheeks, she stumbled into the seat at the back of the boat and plonked her bag next to her. Footsteps pounded on the wooden deck.

'Sorry we're late, but the breakfast is so good here.'

Olivier winked at Aislin. 'You must be Sandra and Jasper. Please sit at the front.'

Ten minutes later, they were out in deeper water and Sandra had stripped down to a skimpy red bikini.

Aislin tugged the sleeves of her fuchsia rashie down to below her wrists and popped a baseball cap on.

'Has anyone told you that look like Amy Jacks?'

Aislin forced a smile in Sandra's direction. 'Yes.'

'Are you Amy?'

'No, sorry.'

Olivier tilted his head towards Aislin. 'Who is this, Amy Jacks?'

Aislin gestured towards Sandra.

'Oh, she's an Australian triple Logie winner. She's in this stunning series *Pure Paradise*.' Sandra slid her sunglasses down her nose and stared straight at Aislin. 'Rumour has it she's separated from her husband and is off to Hollywood.'

Olivier focused on Aislin, 'Have you ever met this, Amy?'

She chuckled and it sounded hollow to her own ears, 'Mate, Sydney is huge.'

'Jasper, don't you agree, this lady is the spitting image of Amy. It makes sense she is here by herself if she's separated and hiding from the media. I mean, who comes to Tahiti by themselves? It's for couples. It's a romantic destination.'

Aislin tried to control her tone. 'Solo travellers are just as entitled to visit a piece of paradise, it's not exclusive to couples.'

'We should start watching out for whales.' Olivier stretched a hand towards her and placed it on Aislin's shoulder. A pleasurable tingling roared through her. He lowered his voice. 'Are you okay? Your marriage broke down only recently, yes?'

Aislin swallowed, 'How did you know?'

'There's a white mark on your wedding finger where a ring has been worn recently.'

She mustered up a nod. Separated for eight months, yet she'd only taken off her wedding ring on the flight here.

'It's still raw, yes.' He scanned her face.

Aislin mustered up a nod.

Olivier pulled his hand away. 'Ladies and gentleman thank you for coming on this tour. This is a new business only two weeks old and so far, we have a one hundred percent success rate of swimming with whales. This is one of the few places in the world that it is permissible to swim with whales. But, sorry there is a but, the whale must be asleep. After a whale does the big dive, they often go to sleep for fifteen minutes. If time permits, we will then snorkel in shallow water with sting rays and black tipped sharks. There are eels in the lagoon, shiny objects attract them. Please remove all your jewellery.'

Aislin twisted at her emerald and diamond claddagh ring on her right hand.

Olivier handed her a small container. 'You can put your ring in here, to keep it safe. Is that the Irish love ring?'

She whispered, 'Yes.'

'Don't close yourself off to love Aislin, it will get easier.'

The heart of the ring pointing towards her wrist symbolised she was in a relationship. Would there ever be a time when she would turn the ring around and announce she was single? Available to have her heart shattered again. There was nothing left to shatter, her heart would never repair.

Aislin slipped the ring back on her hand still relieving how close they'd got to the sleeping whale. It was so big but so gentle. She tugged at the sarong to cover her legs. The sun was unrelenting.

Olivier pulled off his rashie and pegged it to the back of the boat. 'You can dry your top here as well if you like.'

'I'm good, I burn easily.' She reached into her bag and pulled out a tube of suncream.

'Let me help with that.'

She shouldn't. No men. But she held the tube out.

He caressed the blob of suncream on her hand, down her fingers and whispered. 'I hope that you don't think this is too forward, but I would love to take you out for a drink.'

Each touch squeezed oxygen from her, she imagined his fingers elsewhere.

Aislin shuddered and wished they were alone on the boat. So much for no men. She scoured his face with a silent prayer he desired the same. His focus was intense.

She nodded. 'I'm staying in the end bungalow, away from everyone. It's a great spot for watching the sunset. We could have a drink there.'

Sandra sauntered down and haltered any further conversation. Aislin was relieved, what on earth was she thinking inviting a stranger to her bungalow.

A gentle breeze floated through the open doors. The ocean sparkled. Aislin towel dried her hair. A short flowery sleeveless dress showed off her long legs. Not that it mattered, there was no one to impress. Olivier never mentioned drinks again despite the sultry goodbye smile. She could daydream about a holiday romance with him. That was the safest relationship. But the fluttery sensations stirred up earlier were turning into an ache that would be hard to resist if she saw him again. The day bed out on the wooden balcony beckoned to her. She slipped on a pale cotton cardigan before stepping outside. The sky unspoilt of any clouds. A perfect postcard scene.

'*Bonjour.*'

Startled, she moved to the steps. 'Olivier.'

He tied his kayak to a post and took the steps two at a time. 'I come bearing gifts.' He held up a bottle of champagne and two flutes.

The white shirt set off his tan perfectly. *He'd look even better without a shirt.* She shivered. There was no law against a holiday romance. She was going home in four days. 'My favourite.'

'Then I can recommend a French restaurant that is not far from here, they have a Veuve Cliquot theme. He placed the bottle on the table and kissed her on both cheeks.

Olivier smiled. She hadn't misread his earlier looks.

He placed his hands on her shoulders and leant in to kiss her lips.

Everything tingled inside her. She hadn't felt that sensation in years. Seven years ago, Angus had taken her from anguish to euphoria, but everything changed that night.

'I didn't get to tell my story before Sandra butted in. I didn't want you to think that I was hiding anything.'

He's married.

'Before asking you out, I wanted to tell you about my five-year-old son, Nicholas.'

A child. She ran her fingers through her hair. 'Okay.'

'Chloe, his mother walked out on us when he was six months old and for years I questioned what I could have done differently.'

He wants a replacement mum. 'Oh my goodness.'

'Chloe went to live in an art commune in Paris. On her good days she said the best thing we created was Nicholas. On her bad days a cocktail of drugs, she blamed me for forcing her to have a baby and ruining her art career. Her visits became less frequent and then they stopped. Her parents and the police have tried to find her. In the end I thought it best to leave France. My sister and her husband moved to Tahiti years ago. They have three children. I always wanted Nicholas to have siblings.' He nestled closer to her.

Beads of sweat popped along her hairline.

'My dad moved here a year ago and Nicholas and I came six months ago.'

She shouldn't have invited him for a drink.

He stroked her hair. 'The moment I caught sight of you this morning, you took my breath away Aislin. I have not felt that in years and trust me I have been set up on all sorts of dates. Nicholas is the most important person in my life. The best job in the world is being a parent.'

'I can't have children.' Aislin gasped, then cupped her hands over her mouth.

Olivier's body jerked backwards. 'Umh.'

She sunk further into the daybed. Apart from the conversation with her gynaecologist, no one else knew and here she was divulging it to a stranger, who happened to be the sexiest man she'd ever met.

'Aislin, you're deathly pale.'

Her legs wobbled when she forced herself up. 'I don't know why I blurted that out.'

'Let me get us some water.'

She rubbed her eyes and followed him inside. 'Thanks.' She took the glass and sat down on the two-seater lounge.

'Is that why you and your husband separated?'

'Yes. No.' She exhaled. 'No, I never told him.'

Olivier sat down in the single chair to her right. 'What?'

'It's not what you think. I didn't lie to him. Not exactly.' She put the drink down on the coffee table. 'Have you any idea how hard it is to have that conversation. When do you tell someone?'

'Straight away.'

Aislin shook her head, she'd carried this burden of guilt for years. 'The first date. The second date. Before you sleep with them. After you sleep with them.'

She looked at him. Disappointment etched in his face.

'I was twenty when they found an ovarian cyst.'

She picked up the glass and took a large sip. 'My gynaecologist said I had minimal chance of falling pregnant naturally. Even IVF would have an extremely low success rate and to seriously consider did I want to put myself through that stress and expense.'

Aislin stared down at the glass floor next to the coffee table. A school of angelfish darted in and out of view.

'I still can't describe the numbness that drowned me. All my four siblings had kids at that stage. My eldest sister gave birth to twins that same day. That's why I was there on my own, mum rushed to be by Clare's side. Both my parents come from large families. No one ...'

She slammed the tumbler onto the table, 'No one in my family has ever had issues with having children.'

'Aislin ...'

She held her hand up, 'I still feel inadequate, a failure. Ashamed.' She swiped at the tears. 'The evening of my grandparents' sixtieth wedding anniversary, Angus, a mate of my eldest brother, kissed me. I'd had a crush on him for years. I'd dreamt of that moment so many times. I'd already planned my wedding dress and our future children. This was a guy who oozed confidence and didn't shy from awkward conversations. On our first date, he told me he didn't want kids. Suddenly, I didn't have to have that awkward conversation. We were married three months later.'

Aislin stared at her right hand, startled she'd put the ring back on with the heart pointed towards her fingertips. Single and available. Well, Olivier was unlikely to be the next relationship.

Olivier leant forward. 'What went wrong?'

'I was in an accident. No one could reach Angus. My parents went to my house to grab some things for me.' She bit her lip. 'Angus was in bed with my cousin. She's now eight months pregnant and Angus ...' She exhaled. 'He's telling everyone I'm to blame for his affair, that he got tired of me putting my career first over starting a family. Two weeks ago, the divorce was finalised. He wanted it all done before the baby arrived.'

Stillness engulfed the room. She lifted her head. Olivier sat motionless, his eyes looked blank.

'Aislin, I'm so sorry. This accident has left you scarred, has it not? I mean physically.' He pointed to the tube of E gel scar cream on the table.

She nodded. She was delusional that there could be any holiday romance. Even if the pitch darkness hid the sight, he would feel the hideous scar on her arm.

'Don't let your scar, define you.'

She tilted her head to the wooden vaulted ceiling. 'It has. I've lost so much. Even after everything, I still wanted Angus, I was prepared to forgive him. But when he saw my scar, the look on his face wasn't one of horror. That I could have understood. His expression screamed disgust. I moved out that same day. My career came to a halt.'

'Your career?'

'They couldn't work out how to cover up the scar.'

Aislin saw the brief confusion on his face vanish.

'Amy Jacks.'

'That was my acting name. Mine sounded too Irish and producers didn't want an Irish actor.'

Aislin started to remove her cardigan.

'You don't have to show me.'

'I can't keep hiding.' She slipped the cardigan off.

His finger stretched to the long-jagged scar. She held her breath. His touch never came.

'I'm sorry Aislin.'

They sat in silence. There was a crack of thunder. Aislin wanted to cuddle into Olivier's warm body, she needed to know what sorry meant. Sorry for her accident or sorry he couldn't see a future with her. She felt drained telling her story and was afraid to hear his answer. 'I'll understand if you don't want to have that drink.'

Olivier peeped at his watch. 'Champagne doesn't feel right after what you have told me.'

She swallowed, she came with too much baggage for him to explain to his son.

'I should go, before the storm hits.'

Aislin nodded.

He leant over and kissed her on the cheek. 'An early morning swim soon?'

She forced a smile out; he was being polite letting her down gently. 'I'd like that.'

Then he was gone. She sat without moving and the room grew darker. He knew her secret now. If that woman from the tour this morning bleated to the media Amy Jacks was in Tahiti, could she trust him to keep quiet? She hated the media attention, the complete lack of privacy and the expectation that her life belonged to everyone else. Drops of rain tap danced on the wooden balcony. The curtains started to tangle in the wind. The rain turned into a torrential waterfall. She doubted she'd see Olivier again.

A sliver of the sun peeked up on the edge of the water. Then like a bright orange ball it burst up. Tiny dots of pink surrounded the sun. Her second sleepless night since she'd last seen Olivier. Soon would never happen. She should be relieved and stick to her vow of no men. She'd seen his boat go past the resort several times. He could have easily called in. She'd taken to ordering room service for all her meals. Olivier could have sold her story to the media, after all a new business required lots of money.

Aislin sat down at the outside table with her sketch book and flipped through the pages. This is why she'd come to Tahiti, solitude to concentrate on her sketching and writing. She'd captured her profile perched on the wooden deck, legs dangling into the crystal water. The next page she'd tried to sketch Olivier sitting next to her, it hadn't worked. She ripped out the page. *Aislin, no men.*

'*Bonjour* Aislin.'

She jumped and the page fluttered from her hand.

The kayak glided up to the steps.

Breathe. Act casually. '*Bonjour* Olivier. *Ça va?*'

'You speak French.'

'Poorly.'

She stood up and he secured the double kayak to the post.

Olivier bounded up the stairs and leant in to kiss her. Another light kiss. But full of meaning. She swallowed and dropped back into her chair, she was reading too much into a brief kiss. Two days of silence then he just bounced back in. She sighed, perhaps he thought two days was soon.

Olivier sat next to her and picked up the fallen page. 'This is superb, you are very talented Aislin.'

She wanted to rip the drawing up. What would he think of her, drawing the two of them together?

He turned towards her.

She tucked a strand of hair behind her ear. His face was so serious. She pulled the strand of hair back out.

'Aislin, I'm so sorry.'

He didn't need to come to tell her they had no future. She shifted in the chair.

'I should have rung here to let you know I was helping a friend on the mainland. The whale tours are only a month old, so I work part time elsewhere to bring in money.'

'I saw the whale tour boat several times, yesterday and the day before.' She knew she sounded churlish.

'Yes, my dad took the boat out.'

She rubbed her eyes.

'Aislin, you look tired.'

Tears sprung out. 'I haven't slept. I don't know you and I blurted out so many private details.' She buried her face in her hands. 'I thought you might have sold my story to the media.'

'Aislin look at me.' He pried her fingers away and then brushed at her tears.

'I would never do that.' He held up his hands to stop her protests. 'Yes, I see why you could think that. In a way, I was running away from you Aislin. I've always dreamt of a large family and thought that Nicholas should have siblings. I tried to stop thinking about you. That was impossible, you have been in my mind constantly, even in my dreams. I realised I'm content with one child. Nicholas is healthy and happy. I am grateful for that. But ...'

Of course there was a but. She bit down on her lip and tried to control the tears.

'There is something missing from my family circle. Someone to grow old with and someone to help nurture Nicholas. That someone is you Aislin. This is such a cliché, but I believe in love at first sight. Don't go home. Move here.'

Dizziness swept through her, she must have misheard. He wanted her to move to Tahiti? This was madness, they hadn't even gone on a date. 'I don't know what to say. My head feels like a whirlwind.'

'Will this help.' He wrapped her in his arms and kissed her on the lips. She was floating, she hadn't imagined the earlier kiss. The kiss deepened. She could taste the saltiness from his lips.

Aislin pulled away from the kiss. She had to be sensible. 'It's so fast. I don't want to make the same mistake I did with Angus. Then there is Nicholas to consider. He might not be ready to share you. Then there is me, I must learn to trust again.'

Olivier nodded. 'I'm happy with whatever pace you want to go. I just want you in our lives. Tell me that you didn't feel a spark when we first met.'

Aislin inhaled. 'I'm going to need that sketch back.'

'Why?'

'I have to widen the wooden deck to sketch Nicholas in between us.'

SPLEEPØVER

aura gold

Veronica had a head full of shiny, curly auburn hair, that bounced independently into a room before her, framing her bubbly personality. Those who crossed her path never imagined she'd expose herself to this. She was viewed as one of the fortunate.

Cool air drew in the sunset as it reflected in the stained-glass windows. Quiet in its magnificence high above the archway coloured in armouring white stone. An impressive turret reached to the sky. Embellished with swirling circular pane glass, a yellow brick porch welcomed her as if to embrace all whom entered.

As she lowered her head from the view, she stepped up from the footpath. One, two, three, four. The steps rose up to the grand wooden doors. Her determined feet stamped down followed by arms stretching upright to the sky in a grandiose fashion. 'I'll spend the night here.'

Her eyes scrolled her phone, as the light fell across her face. Her thoughts turned to Ben as she settled, realised it was time to sign off.

Dismissing the thought of feeling alone she snuggled up with her favourite blankey and a talisman. She held them tight with the view they would protect her from the night shadows. Veronica soon sank into the night, thoughts trolled her, should anything untoward happen. Sighing out the fear, she shuffled her feet and slid worm like to find the most embracing position.

She wanted to keep her eyes open, but slumber rolled over her eyelids and closed them shut.

The next morning, David tried a gentle rock. He saw eyes flicker behind lids through tousled hair.

'Hello! Hello! Hello,' David said somewhat louder, beckoning with each hello, 'I need to open the doors.' He rolled the body away as it was wedged against the door.

'Another homeless person, that's three this week,' he muttered under his breath.

The woman rolled over to face him. Brushed the hair from her face.

His dry mouth uttered sheepishly, 'You're awake!'

A quiet satisfied smile lifted her lips as she took in the sight of him. 'What? Yes.' Her eyes squinted from the bright light of day as she unzipped the top of the sleeping bag open.

David fell silent fumbling in his pocket searching for the key to open the chapel door.

With a gentle pointed toe he stepped over her finding his footing at the same time politely gesturing for her to come inside. She gathered up the sleeping bag around her and jumped like she was in a potato sack race to the pew he was sitting on.

'Would you like a cup of tea?'

David watched her roll down the sleeping bag to her waist as she leant the top half of her body into him. With a cheeky tone she said, 'That will be lovely. Must be talking to mwah Angel! Ye must be mwah guardian angel.'

His conscious mind took over. He wondered who this well-groomed woman was. He hadn't seen her before. With a deep sigh, he cast his eyes down to avoid her lack of reserve. 'Tea it is and something to eat?'

As she shook her tossed hair, she responded with delight. 'White no sugar please.' He slowly panned her new sleeping bag and her manicured hands before standing up. He turned on his heels as if on a mission. As he quietly disappeared to the tearoom, he heard her yell out behind him, 'I'm Veronica.' in a breathy, deep staccato voice, '... nice to meet you.'

On return, he interrupted her gazing up at the ceiling. She was picturing him as an angel, big brown eyes to fall deeply into, dressed only with large, white wings. His energy was like he wasn't human. He reached out with the cup and dispelled her fantasy as he introduced himself, 'I'm David.' And added he was the new trainee minister.

As she touched his hand, there was an electric shock between them as the tea rose out of the cup as if on a water ride at a fun park.

'Nearly!' they said in unison.

'Snap,' they said together, giggling, Then raised their pinkie finger like children.

Her shoulders twitched as she thought to herself, *I like his energy.*

She paused, took a gulp of tea. Angled her body towards him. With a low yet upbeat voice she filled the silence. 'First time for everything.' They shared laughs about the absurdity.

He opened a packet of sweet strawberry-flavoured biscuits.

'Would you like another tea.'

She nodded as if her head was going to roll off her shoulders. 'Yes, yes.' Wanting more of whatever this was. She sat in silence took in her surrounds, gathered her feelings she felt echoed within the chapel. Veronica laid her bedding on the floor and put on a bright orange shirt. Her thoughts pounced under her breath as she hummed the tune from 'Silent Night'. This was the moment she came to the reality David was truly a man of the cloth.

As if hypnotised she watched him do a dance move in time with the tune she hummed. She smiled at him as he balanced two cups of tea without spilling a drop.

This time their hands lingered longer when he passed her the cup. There was an unspoken connection. Most of the day passed and she knew she had another night out in her homeless bag. That wasn't important to her now, even though she was under contract. She was aware her phone had been vibrating on silent for the past five hours.

Veronica felt David had an ulterior motive and wasn't letting her out of his sight as he said, 'I'm feeling hungry, how about you? Let's grab a soup from around the corner, it has a beautiful outdoor area in the sunshine.'

'Yes, let's do it,' she said ignoring the continuous *brrrr* vibration in her bag.

Surround sound of rattling plates and voices from many different people gave them a background for their conversation.

It was as if none of the ambiance existed. Hungry smiles shared in the moment she lifted the spoon to her lips.

With grace, Veronica placed the spoon back in the soup bowl, turned to him and grabbed his other hand. Her arm moved with great care around his neck and pulled him close towards her as if to tell him a secret. His neck skin was so soft and almost translucent. She thought that her hand would go through him. Wondering at the same time what his vows were, she whispered to his ear, 'For a moment I thought you were God and I should confess.'

He pulled back as he laughed. 'Yes, tis me, in the flesh.'

'Seriously David, I need to tell you something. I'm—'

Terse words ricocheted behind them. Shooting them apart. 'We've been looking for you everywhere.' Ben's voice was loud and stern. A silent hush echoed around the Soup kitchen. She gripped David's hand tighter. Ben raised his voice again in disapproval. 'Veronica, unbelievable.'

She turned to the three very tall, unshaven men, who surrounded her carrying camera and sound equipment. Ben, who headed the TV crew, puffed out his frustration.

'We need to set the shot.' Ben stated in a solemn manner. The crew followed his direction. Ben pointed at Veronica as he moved around the table to eyeball her and berate her for not being at the last location.

The cameraman pitched the camera on his shoulder as the voice recorder plunged the large fluffed up microphone in David's face to separate them.

Ben stood, arms folded, with angry rapid fire, sprayed his questions. 'What's all this about Veronica? What's going on?'

Veronica felt as if she was trapped in another dimension, almost as if these men were aliens with weapons to destroy her. 'How rude and intrusive,' she said under her breath.

David heard her words. Bewildered, he stood up shaking the table with the soup rolling back and forth in the bowl, tsunami style. In a protective stance and firm voice David said, 'Who are you?'

Looking directly at Veronica, Ben's chest pushed out the words. 'Well, who the hell are you?' Directing his question to her as he pointed at David.

David picked up on his tone and sensed there was history between them. His eyes turned to the red light of the camera and realised he was being filmed.

Before she could lift her head from between her hands to intervene, David pushed his chair back. Charged with his energy, it fell to the floor. Flabbergasted he turned to face Veronica. 'What is going on here? Have you set me up? You betrayed my compassion and trust.'

With the camera still rolling, David reached his hand towards the lens and moved his body in an angular fashion to extricate himself from the viewfinder and the table.

Veronica was speechless. By the time she got to mouth her words he was gone like the wind. Only the last bit of his upset energy was left for her to hold onto. She finally came to her senses and asked Ben to stop the camera roll.

Ben continued to fire off questions in succession whilst he picked up the chair to sit next to her.

'Veronica, who was that man? Tell me what is going on? Why haven't you answered your phone?' demanded Ben. Deafening silence surrounded them. She looked back down at the table and saw her surrounds in slow motion. The soup bowls were together and somehow David's spoon was in her bowl.

She couldn't speak, she didn't know what to say, didn't know what to do. She wanted to run after him. David's words kept tonguing in her now thumping head, *You betrayed me*. The tune from a Marianne Faithfull song 'Come and Stay with Me' popped into her mind.

Work was everything to Veronica, what would the boss think if this got back to him.

'Do you know which beach shelter I am sleeping in tonight?' Her tone caustic as she threw her arms up in the air as if to surrender. 'Final night right!'

David returned to the chapel somewhat out of breath, fumbled for his keys and spied her brand-new sleeping bag in the corner. He had allowed her to stay in God's home, a shelter from the cold and the dangers of street life. He grabbed her belongings and tossed them out onto the street.

Since his marriage break up, he'd had trouble trusting people. His divorce dragged through the courts for years, lost his job and became homeless. David found peace and solace as a trainee minister. This work with the homeless was a challenge but rewarding. However, this betrayal hit him hard, and his actions created an overwhelming sense of anxiety. Taking a few deep breaths to settle down, he was surprised by his strong emotions. As he became mindful, more present, he sat in his favourite recliner chair and began to examine his feelings. It was a comfort being with Veronica, a feeling he had not felt in years.

To distract himself, he switched the television on. He flicked through the channels until he stopped on a documentary titled: *Sleepover, My Night Out*. David moved closer to the TV, bent down and held tight onto its frame.

'I gave up many a good night's sleep,' Veronica said as her image flashed on the television screen. 'I wanted to bring attention to the plight of the homeless in our city and find out why rough sleeper numbers were so high. There are many sites across the city filled with mattresses, tarpaulins, cardboard, and all sorts of material the homeless use to protect themselves as best they can. Sheltering on the streets is described by the social service groups as a catastrophe. I chose to step up, help, in any way. I spent five days sleeping in the streets and heard of the work done by a trainee minister and decided to see for myself.'

Veronica's voice came loud and clear through the television.

She also came to his thoughts every day since they met. He had no peace. He liked her playful expressions and touch ever since she had his hand in hers. Smiling he thought, *I need to find her.*

The chapel was full of many different coloured flowers. David stood at the end of the isle delivering the daily prayers. Veronica had visited many times in disguise, without being recognised. She called the chapel most days and left messages for him with her contact number, but David did not return her calls. She wanted to be close to him again and listen to his silken voice. Share her heartfelt truth. She had never felt energy like she had with him and felt he was her destiny.

Inside the chapel, she enjoyed the sense of community and the stories, how they related to one's life. 'I wonder why I missed out on these reflective Sundays,' she whispered to an elderly woman, stylishly dressed in white as she wiggled herself in the pew. 'It's not all doom and gloom. Good positive hope for everyone to takeaway. Best of all I get to have a sing song.'

But she couldn't keep up these incognito visits any longer, she had to face him. Her mind told her to ask for his forgiveness. If that didn't work, she would lay down in front of him like a sacrifice. She would do anything to turn him around. Veronica remained seated on the pew, listened for the door to close after everyone had left. She was unsure how to make the next move and whether it would be welcomed. Before she worked up enough courage to open her mouth to let him know she loved the service, he walked back into the chapel. She rose to her feet to greet him. Their eyes met and searched each other's soul.

'I know the truth Veronica,' he said pleading. 'I am so very sorry I jumped to conclusions. I was hurt.'

She moved towards him and reached out, took both of his hands. She remembered the first time she took his hands as tears rolled from deep wells in her eyes. Amongst the sobs, he said, 'How could I be so stupid and ignore you and my feelings for you, only to give you silence.'

Veronica spoke to him in a calm soft voice, turned her lips to his and purposefully missed them to kiss him on the side of the cheek. She pulled back from him to take him in. It was hard to leave him.

They led each other to the front doors. David opened his arms wide to give her permission to lean into him. After looking around, as if God was watching, he planted his lips passionately upon hers as they fell hard against the unlocked door. It fell open along with them splayed on top of each other at the entrance. Laughing she blurted out, 'I've missed you, David.' She placed her arms around his neck to hold him firm and said, 'I'm in heaven.'

Laughter echoed in God's ears as they closed the chapel doors behind them.

GOING THE DISTANCE

Kate Kelsen

The wind whipped along Marine Parade as Joy searched for the vegetarian café. She found it closed, and doubt flooded her mind—was this the right place? She took out her phone and tried to open the dating app—it had been crashing all morning, and she and Monty hadn't exchanged phone numbers yet.

She did not want a repeat of what happened with the last dating app match. She had planned to meet Stephen in his suburb of Burleigh Heads. Joy thought they were meeting at the northern end of The Esplanade, but he insisted it was the southern end they had agreed on. He wasn't willing to walk the two kilometres, so she walked to meet him, finding him disgruntled and ready to leave. She unmatched him on the way home.

'Joy?'

A tall man with dark, curly hair and glasses approached. He wore shorts, a T-shirt and a striped scarf. She sighed with relief—he looked like his profile picture, which had caught her eye immediately on the app. They hugged, and Monty looked at the closed café.

'Well, I don't think the vegetarian place exists anymore. Shall we find an alternative?'

'Sure.' Joy shivered, pulling her jacket closed. 'Aren't you cold?'

'No.' Monty laughed. 'I'm English.'

Two blocks over, they found another café, its outdoor seating area walled in by plastic wind barriers.

'They don't seem to have vegetarian options,' Monty said, 'It's all right, I'll have a coffee.'

'How long have you been vegetarian?' Joy enquired.

'Twenty years.'

They placed their orders, and the getting-to-know-you chat began.

'What kind of music do you like?' asked Monty.

'Lots of different types,' said Joy. 'I've loved Olivia Newton–John since I was a teenager. After I saw *Grease*, I bought my first pair of denim jeans and got a perm.'

Monty chuckled. 'You rebel!'

'What about you?'

'I love rock and roll …' Monty sang the line from the song. 'But I'm a fan of world music. Have you heard of Deep Forest?'

'I love Deep Forest.'

When their food arrived, Monty studied Joy's order.

'It looks good.'

'We can share this if you like.' Joy pushed the plate closer and waved down the waiter, who delivered a second fork. Monty popped a piece of quiche in his mouth.

'Mmm, it's good.'

'So, what did you do for work before you retired?'

'I was an Art and English teacher. These days I volunteer at a second-hand bookshop a few days a week. The rest of the time, I'm writing.'

'Do you still paint?'

'Occasionally.'

Joy sat forward, resting her chin in her hand. 'What is your novel about?'

'It's a thriller. I'm taking a break from it and working on a short story. A comedy. I can read it to you when it's finished, and you can tell me if it's funny.' Monty leant forward, holding Joy's gaze. 'I'd love to read one of your poems.'

Joy's heart fluttered.

Droplets of rain plonked onto their plates, and they laughed as they shuffled their chairs under the cover of the café's roof. Joy's foot brushed Monty's.

'Sorry.'

Monty winked, and said, 'Don't be sorry.'

When the rain stopped, they took the opportunity to walk along the Coolangatta foreshore.

'Do you have children, Joy?'

'My daughter Rosie lives here on the Gold Coast. What about you?'

'I have a daughter, too. Ky. She's eighteen. She lives with me in Lismore.'

A light mist of rain dusted their faces.

'We're not having much luck with the weather,' said Monty. 'Perhaps we should call it a day.'

Joy's heart sank; she was just starting to like Monty. Was this it? The butterflies of excitement were dampened by the rain.

'I'll walk you to the bus stop,' Monty offered.

As they walked, Monty's hand was so close Joy could reach out and grab it, touch the energy brewing between them. Hold onto him so he didn't slip away. The bus stop was in sight — it was now or never. Joy extended her fingers, but quickly clenched them into a fist.

Huddled under the shelter, Monty turned to her.

'I guess we'll chat on the app.'

He leant in, his embrace lingering a few moments longer this time, sending tingles through Joy's body. She waved as he dashed to the carpark.

On the bus, Joy's adrenaline fizzled out, but her thoughts kept ticking over. What had Monty thought of her? She shouldn't care, as it was only a first date. But she did.

Back at Rosie's house, Joy's phone lay dormant. In the late afternoon, she took Rosie's dogs for a walk to take her mind off the anticipation. If she wanted to brave the dating world again, she had to be prepared to face multiple rejections with her head held high. She dreaded starting the dating process over again with someone else. Her time was precious and could easily be wasted catching buses and trains all over the place for dates that led nowhere.

That evening, Rosie bounced into the house after work.

'How did it go?' she probed.

Joy laughed at her comic enthusiasm.

'It went well. We were rained out, though.'

'What's he like?'

'He's a true hippie, straight out of the seventies.'

'Are you going on another date?'

'I don't know. I haven't heard from him.'

'Well, don't you dare message him first!'

The next morning, Joy waited for the train back to Brisbane. Her phone pinged. It was a notification from the dating app.

Monty sent you a message.

The hum of nerves intensified as she opened it.

Maybe we should try again another day.

Her anxiety flipped into excitement once again. She typed a reply, smiling until her cheeks hurt.

I'd like that.

For their second date, they planned to meet in Murwillumbah, a township just south of the Queensland–New South Wales border. The outlook from the bus window offered Joy views of the ocean in one direction and Mount Warning in the other. Rolling hills were dotted with grazing cows, with banana and sugarcane plantations rising tall in the valley. The bus descended into the quaint village of Tumbulgum, and onto Murwillumbah.

Tweed Regional Gallery and Margaret Olley Arts Centre were two kilometres outside the town centre. Joy powerwalked along the stretch of road, beads of sweat dripping down her forehead. This was not the kind of 'hot and sweaty' she had envisioned for a date. Monty was waiting when she arrived. They hugged, and Joy hoped she didn't smell.

'Did you walk from town?' Monty asked.

'Yes,' Joy panted. 'The bus company in Murwillumbah is different to the one in Tweed Heads. They only take cash. I found an ATM in town, but I tried to put my pin number in too many times and my card was blocked.'

'You should have called,' said Monty. 'I would have picked you up.'

'Thank–you. I don't mind walking, I just didn't think it was going to get so hot so quickly.'

'So you don't have a car,' Monty commented.

'No, I haven't for a while. It's an expense I can live without.'

Behind the positive reframing lurked the truth. She wanted a car, but money was tight being a single woman over sixty.

They spent two hours exploring the gallery and arts centre. Back in town, they passed fresh food stores, bakeries, cafés, and restaurants, closed and boarded up. A stark reminder of the flooding which devastated the township in February and March the previous year. Stains still marked the art deco façades, showing where the water had risen.

With the limited options available, Monty struggled to find something to eat. Joy's stomach rumbled as they walked past the eateries, her hunger chewing away at her patience. She was relieved when Monty settled for scones and a coffee.

'Did you like the gallery?' he asked.

'Very much,' said Joy. 'Margaret Olley was an amazing woman. Painting until she died. I want to be like that when I'm eighty-eight. Writing my poetry at home.'

Joy noticed a smudge of jam in the corner of Monty's mouth.

'Here, you've got something ...'

In a daring moment, she reached to wipe it away. How she longed to reach further and run her hands through his dark, luscious curls. Monty leant into her touch, perching his chin in his hand.

'So, how long have you been single?' he asked.

'Four years,' said Joy, pulling her hand back. 'You?'

'The same.'

'Were you married?'

'No,' Monty scoffed. 'Never married. What about you?'

'Yes.'

'It must be strange for an adult child when their parents separate. How did Rosie take it?'

'Oh, it wasn't from her dad.'

'You've been married twice?'

Joy's gaze dropped; she didn't want to see Monty's reaction. 'Three times.'

There it was. The biggest of her secret shames. She dared to look at him: he sat back, his eyebrows raised.

'Well, you've beat me out of the park.'

It started to rain, dampening their plans of exploring Murwillumbah. Monty pulled his phone out.

'Excuse me a moment.'

He stepped away from the table to answer the call.

'Is everything all right?' Joy asked when he returned.

'It's my daughter. What time is your bus?'

'Two o'clock,' said Joy.

'How much is a ticket?'

'Two dollars fifty.'

'I've got coins.'

'Are you sure?' Embarrassment flushed hot in Joy's cheeks. 'You don't have to.'

'I insist.'

The conversation fell quiet on the walk to the bus stop. On the way home, Joy ruminated over the day. She'd gone and done it now. She had said too much too soon.

At Rosie's house, she collapsed onto the couch, exhausted. Flawed by the emotional contrasts of excitement, apprehension, and doubt. Rosie handed her a glass of wine, and Joy took a generous sip.

'I told Monty about my marriages.'

'And?'

'He seemed shocked.'

'Pfft.' Rosie rolled her eyes. 'He shouldn't care.'

'Well, people do.'

'Who?'

'Aunty Jane and Aunty Elizabeth.'

'And look at their marriages. At least you don't stay when you're unhappy. Monty should be worried about what you think. You might say he's inexperienced for having never been married!'

Joy laughed.

'I just keep thinking, I'm sixty-two, I don't have a car, I rent a room in my brother's house and I only work a few hours a week.'

'Don't be so hard on yourself, Mum. You lost everything when you left Ed. You're rebuilding, and it takes time.'

Joy nodded.

'I do really like Monty. He's intelligent, and his enthusiasm is refreshing. Your dad, Greg, and Ed were never interested in museums and art galleries. I've never been able to talk about writing with a man like I can with Monty. We have so much in common.'

'Well, it sounds like you're onto something good, Mum.'

Joy's quest for love began a year after her first divorce. She met a carpet salesman named Greg while accompanying her elderly parents to church. His personality had been as exciting as his profession, and he wore socks with sandals. But he was a sensible, church–going man, the kind her father approved of.

Greg's efforts in the getting–to–know–you process had been underwhelming. Nothing about Joy seemed to catch his interest, even her poetry. She was surprised when he asked her on a second date. She suspected his shyness had gotten the better of him and decided to give him another shot. Their marriage lasted two years.

She met Ed while having lunch at a restaurant by herself. They were married two years later. He was a DJ and dreamt of taking a motorhome on a working holiday around Australia. He convinced Joy to sell her home to buy the vehicle. On the road between gigs, they listened to live music and danced the nights away.

Joy loved Ed's passion, but her efforts were not reciprocated. When she mentioned writing a new poem, he changed the subject. Sometimes, she'd wondered if he even heard her speak. She travelled thousands of kilometres in support of Ed's nomadic dream. After five years, she had stopped going the distance for him. Ed kept the motorhome in the divorce.

When Joy was ready to find love again, Rosie suggested online dating. Despite her reservations, Joy agreed to try it. The app's in-depth compatibility test was designed to give a deeper insight into Joy's character. She worked through eighty questions on personality type, likes and dislikes, communication style, and motivations. Some of the questions were strange: one showed a series of paired images and asked her to choose a favourite. How did this choice impact her love life? And what about the "algorithm" controlling her future happiness? How times had changed!

Joy summarised herself in two-hundred-and-twenty-seven characters:

Avid reader. Writer of poetry and songs. Enjoys gardening and cooking, listening to music, and playing piano and guitar.

Adventurous—loves day trips, road trips, and weekend getaways. Looking for someone to come on the journey.

The app churned out match recommendations, and the possibilities were endless. Joy sifted through dozens of profiles, but instead of finding the information she needed, she filtered through criteria she didn't care much about. She hadn't felt a spark with someone by knowing their height or level of education. But the more she used the app, the more detail it had on her, which was meant to make the algorithm work better. The search had eventually led her to Monty.

For their third date, Joy suggested spending the weekend in Lismore. She had planned to book an Airbnb room in Lennox Head, on the coast between Byron Bay and Ballina, but Monty suggested she stay with him.

'Ky can spend the night at her mum's or a friend's place,' he insisted.

Nervous excitement flittered in her heart as Joy considered Monty's invitation. This was a quantum leap—it was one thing to ride in his car, and another to stay at his house. They hadn't even kissed yet, and now she was going to spend the night. What were his intentions? His expectations?

Monty was at the bus station when she arrived.

'How long did it take you to get here?' he asked.

'Five hours.'

'You've been travelling since 6 am?'

'I wanted to get here as early as possible.'

'Well, from now on, why don't I pick you up from Ballina, and drop you to the bus in Tweed Heads. It will save you some miles.'

'Okay.' Joy nodded. 'I'd appreciate that.'

'Well, you do all these miles for me, I can do a few for you.'

From the passenger seat, Joy looked out the window. Like Murwillumbah, Lismore had been hit hard by the 2022 floods. Many businesses were still boarded up.

'It's like a ghost town,' she commented. 'Even after a year.'

'People moved away,' said Monty. 'They had barely recovered when the second flood hit. It was too costly to rebuild. But some have stuck it out. At the bookshop, we've put the cooking equipment and white goods on platforms. It can all be quickly raised off the ground if it floods again. And we're leaving the walls bare brick or concrete, so the plaster won't rot if water gets in.'

'You're doing things differently this time.' Joy looked at Monty. 'It must have been a shock to learn I've been married three times.'

Monty nodded.

'I was surprised, but only because I've never been married.' He laughed. 'I can't imagine what it must be like to do it three times.'

'I was raised in a strict religion, you see. No one in my family has been divorced. I was ashamed to be living with a partner outside marriage.'

'You don't have to explain yourself, Joy. I know lots of people who have been divorced more than once. It's common nowadays, especially at our age. And anyway, who am I to judge?' He smiled, reaching for her hand across the centre console. 'I still can't believe you travelled five hours to see me.'

'I always have plenty to do on the way. I wrote a whole new poem this morning.'

'I'd like to hear it.'

Stepping into the bookshop café, Joy gasped her delight at the eclectic, old-world art deco furniture and printing relics.

'This place looks like something you'd find in Melbourne!'

They approached the counter and both ordered toasties.

Students from the nearby university studied at the tables. Others played board games. While they waited for their toasties, Joy browsed the bookshelves lining the walls floor to ceiling. Above their heads fairy lights hung from the rafters. After they had finished eating, Monty sipped his coffee as he listened to Joy read her poem. Glancing at him between verses, she noted the gentle adoration in his gaze.

'I sit across the table from you.
Sipping on tea, the ambience, the hue
My ears are listening, my eyes beholding
Yet my thoughts are wildly racing.

A wave of emotion floods through me
As you chatter about music and movies
Your hair brushed back, your long curls black
Sit softly against the nape of your neck.

My breath slows to stay composed
Sitting still with a ladylike poise
Yet I want to jump up and interrupt
Straddle your lap and bridge this gap.

But it's too soon in our acquaintance
To show my passion unrestrained.
Appearances may deceive some
But I know a gentleman when I see one.

It's not just your looks, your style, your smile
It's also the things you do and say
You're thoughtful and gentle way
Your passion to live like it's your last day.

It's the moments when we connect
In common likes and interests
It's the times you make me laugh
At your jokes and impersonated drama.

I'm aroused, I'm curious, I'm intrigued
I want to show you more of me
As I look around your environment
Maybe next time I'll show myself unrestrained.'

She lowered the piece of paper, noting Monty's cheeky smile.
'Would you like to come home with me?' he purred.

The next day, the kilometres slipped by too quickly under the tyres as Monty drove Joy to Tweed Heads. They waited together, and as the bus approached, he pulled her close and kissed her. They continued to hold each other as the other passengers boarded.

'How about I come up to Brisbane next weekend?' said Monty.

'That would be lovely,' Joy breathed.

She smiled through her sadness as she waved to Monty from the bus window. She was going blissfully mad. Every moment spent apart was unbearable, and every moment spent together was never enough.

Standing in King George Square, I looked around for the familiar head of curly hair.

The poem formulated in her mind as she waited outside City Hall, listening to the dial tone ring. Monty answered.

'I'm on my way. I've ended up on Petrie Terrace. I'm still getting used to Google Maps.'

When he arrived, Joy greeted him with a hug and kiss.

'So, what's the plan for today?' asked Monty.

'There's a record shop in Queen Street Mall I think you'll like.'

The walls of Rocking Horse Records were plastered with tour posters. Every square inch of the shop was packed full of CDs, vinyls, T-shirts, music books, magazines, and posters. Monty's grin was as big as the record he was holding.

After combing through the shop's collections, they crossed the Brisbane River to Southbank, where they explored the art galleries marvelling at paintings, photographs, and sculptures.

201

Joy's stomach grumbled in anticipation of the lengthy search for suitable dining options.

'I looked up restaurants in South Bank,' said Monty. 'I found an Italian place on Grey Street with vegetarian options. Their menu looks delicious.'

Joy relaxed with relief. Monty's proactive approach to the day's dining options was a pleasant surprise.

After lunch, Monty pulled out a piece of paper.

'I finished my short story.'

'Congratulations!'

'Would you like to hear it?'

'Fire away.'

Monty cleared his throat.

'Samantha and Jake's first date unfolded like a sitcom pilot. They decided on a quaint comedy club, hoping for a night of laughter. Little did they know, the universe had its own comedic script. The comedian happened to be Jake's ex-roommate, Phil, who never missed a chance to embarrass him. Phil, sensing the awkwardness, called them out. "Look who's here! Jake, the guy who still thinks socks with sandals are a fashion statement!"

'Amidst uproarious laughter, Jake turned tomato-red, while Samantha giggled uncontrollably. In a twist of fate, the waiter accidentally spilt water on Jake's lap, launching him into an impromptu interpretive dance. Samantha was in stitches. This date was a comedy goldmine.'

Monty looked at Joy.

'I take your laughter as positive feedback.'

'I liked the socks and sandals remark.'

Monty's phone rang, and he stepped away.

'Is everything all right?' Joy asked when he returned to the table.

'Ky's in a packing frenzy. She starts university on the Gold Coast next week.'

'So, will you stay in Lismore now she's leaving?'

'I haven't thought about it.' He winked at her. 'I could move to the Gold Coast too, and be close to both of you.' He reached across the table and took Joy's hands. 'I best be heading off soon. Get back to Ky. I'm sorry. It feels like we've had so little time together today.'

Joy sighed her disappointment.

'Yes, it does.'

Heavy rain started as they walked back across the river, huddled underneath Joy's umbrella.

'Do you think you'll live in Brisbane long-term?' Monty asked.

'I don't think so,' said Joy. 'I only moved here because my marriage ended. My brother had a spare room.'

'It must have been hard starting over three times.'

'It was. I've had to let go of a lot of things, and people. But I feel a lot lighter now.'

'Where would you move?'

'The Gold Coast maybe, to be closer to Rosie.' Joy grinned. 'I've been considering Northern New South Wales, too. It's so beautiful, and I've felt for a while that I would end up there someday.'

They approached Roma Street surrounded by football fans marching toward Suncorp Stadium. A sea of team colours and umbrellas swarmed past them in the opposite direction. They stopped outside the train station, laughing.

'That was crazy!' Monty exclaimed.

Joy looked at the departure screen.

'There's a train in ten minutes.'

'You'd better dash.'

The busyness of the city fell away around them as they kissed. The noise, the people rushing past. The time that was constantly slipping away from them stopped. Monty pulled Joy close, and the distance they were about to put between them dissipated.

.

CONTRIBUTORS

R. A. PURTILL has been involved in the writing community in Brisbane since 2012. Her short stories have been published in local and national anthologies. She is studying a Bachelor of Creative Industries, majoring in Creative Writing and  Publishing at the Petrie campus of the University of the Sunshine Coast. This has given her a broad interest across many genres. She enjoys science fiction, fantasy, historical fiction, biography, and creative non-fiction.

She facilitates the Strathpine Writers Group, a monthly meeting of keen and varied wordsmiths, and she is a frequent writing conference and retreat attendee.

When she is not working on assessments for university or writing her steampunk dragon fantasy, she enjoys multi-media art, a brisk walk around the block and coffee with friends.

You can find Raelene at

facebook.com/PurtillWriter/

RITA MACLEAN lives in a tin shack by the sea, catching seagulls she uses to make delicious pies, and writing weird stories. She likes going for long bicycle rides with her cat, who always wears aviator goggles to stop her whiskers blowing  up into her eyes as they speed down to the beach to search for mermaid eggs.

Rita writes offbeat and fantastical tales for kids and young adults as Martii Maclean. To find out more about Rita (and her alto-ego Martii), and access free resources for kids and teachers, reach out through LinkedIn and social media, or by emailing her.

You can find Rita at

kookycatbooks@gmail.com

GARY DAVID is an emerging writer and has always loved the art of storytelling, and how we learn and grow through it. It may have started when he was reading stories to his foster children, or teaching kids to read in prison, or even living  in remote areas working in community development programs.

He spends most of his time in outback Australia in any number of humanitarian projects, whether it is refugees or indigenous or other needed programs. He has received a number of awards for his work.

With degrees in criminology and psychology, his interests have always lain in adventures that have taken him through third world regions across six different continents.

Gary has a love of adventure that he is looking forward to bringing to the world of both fiction and nonfiction writing.

His published works include 'Last Kill and Testament' in *Meanwhile Murder* and 'Butterfly' in *Charms of Love*.

You can find Gary at

garydavid.com.au

ROBIN MARTIN THOMAS is an author and teacher, who writes both adult and young adult romance. Originally from Canada, she now lives in Moreton Shire with her husband and crazy little Pomeranian, who is often by her side when she writes.

Her YA sci-fi romance series, *The Alien Chronicles* includes *My Alien, The Alien Within,* and *Once an Alien.* Her most recent YA book is *Finding Gilbert,* a paranormal, historical story set in South East Queensland.

Adult books include the *Short Sweetz* series of romantic comedies, *High Stakes* and *Bonjour Cherie.*

A member of Write-Links, for children's and YA writers, she has also attended many Rainforest Writers' Retreat workshops over the years, and has short stories in several of their anthologies. Robin also connects with writers and readers on her author's Facebook page or on her website.

You can find Robin at

robinmartinthomas.com
Facebook @robinmartinthomas

SARAH HEGERTY is a speculative fiction writer, wife, mum, gamer, and adventure seeker who just wants some sleep. Living in sunny Queensland, Australia, she spends her time fantasising about snow-covered mountains in cooler climates.

Her published works include Anthologies 'Playing the System' in *Seven Deadly Sins: Avarice*, 'Living Next Door to Amy'in *Seven Deadly Sins: Lust*, 'The Six' in *Short Stories of Forest and Fantasy*, 'Ghost Trap' in *Short Stories of Ghosts and Graves*, 'Carpe Diem' in *Short Stories of Science and Space*, and 'Dangerous Frontiers' in *Got Game?*

Although she spends a lot of time writing short stories, she does hope to have longer works published one day.

You can find Sarah at

www.sarahhegerty.com

JEANETTE O'HAGAN has spun tales in the world of Nardva from the age of eight. She enjoys writing fantasy, sci-fi, poetry, and editing. Her Nardvan stories span continents, millennia and cultures. Some involve courtly intrigue, shapeshifters and  magic. Others include plasma rifles, space stations, and cyborgs.

She has published over forty stories and poems, including the *Under the Mountain Series* (5 books), *Ruhanna's Flight and Other Stories*; *Akrad's Children* and *Rasel's Song*, the first two books in the *Akrad's Legacy* series; and recently stories in the *Starlit Realms: Fantasy Anthology* and *A Glimmer of Uncommon Fairy Tales*.

Jeanette lives in Brisbane. She has practised medicine, studied communication, history, theology and has a Master of Arts (Writing). She loves painting, travel, catching up for coffee with friends, pondering the meaning of life. She is also an avid reader and enjoys tracking down family tree conundrums.

You can find Jeanette at

jeanetteohagan.com
Facebook @JeanetteOHaganAuthorAndSpeaker

ROBIN ADOLPHS is a published author of eighteen children's picture books and director of Butternut Books. In 2019, Robin published her first middle grade fiction, *Princes of Aranmore*. In 2022, she published the first four books in *Mookie's Adventures on Earth* series. Book Five due for release end of 2023.

Robin also writes poetry and short stories, '2084' in *Short Stories of Science and Space* (2021) and 'The Nemesis' *Got Game* (2023). In this anthology, *Charms of Love*, Robin chose her love of poetry to write 'Within the Fire'.

Robin's love of picture books comes from her background in Early Childhood Education and she has taught in Victoria, Queensland, and Germany. Her love of poetry she credits to her father who read poetry to her mother.

A highlight for Robin was her inclusion in the Australian Publishers Association contingent at the Frankfurt Book Fair in 2019. Commissioned in 2016 to write a book for young children on Domestic Abuse by the National Rural Women's Coalition. And 'Brave Danny' was born.

In 2021, 'Pirates Don't Read' was shortlisted for the 2021 Speech Pathology Awards Australia.

You can find Robin at

robinadolphs.com or butternutbooks.com
Facebook @ Children's Author Robin Adolphs

LEA SCOTT is a crime thriller writer who has independently published three novels, *The Ned Kelly Game* (2009), *Eclipsed* (2010) and *One for All* (2013).

Her short stories have been published in numerous anthologies. Lea's work has been longlisted for the Fish Short Story (UK) prize, the Richell Prize with Hachette and the Adaptable competition with Queensland Writers Centre and Screen Queensland, and she received an Editor's Choice Award for her short story 'Final Play' in the RWR anthology *Got Game?*

Lea holds a PhD in Creative Writing and worked for five years as a lecturer in creative writing at Central Queensland University, served as the Chair of the Queensland Writers Centre, and now owns the iconic Rosetta Books in the magical Sunshine Coast hinterland town of Maleny.

You can find Lea at

leascott.com

EMMA RENNISON is a British-Australian author and mother of two children diagnosed with multiple epiphyseal dysplasia and scoliosis. She has one bionic hip and writes about her family's experiences of disability, and works of fiction.

Her first published story, 'No Guts, No Glory', won the 2020 Editor's Choice Award in the RWR anthology, *Short Stories of Science and Space*. She was runner-up in The Jennifer Burbidge Prize 2021 and shortlisted for the Newcastle Short Story Award 2021. In 2022, she had a memoir piece published on SBS Voices as part of their Emerging Writers' Competition, and was shortlisted for the City of Melbourne Lord Mayor's Creative Writing Awards.

Emma was selected as a Writers Victoria Writeability Fellow in 2022 and is currently working on her first novel.

You can find Emma at

emmarennison.com
Instagram @emmajrennison
Facebook @emmarennisonauthor

JENNY WOOLSEY, M.Ed. (Hons), is an author, potter, speaker, carer and disability advocate. Jenny's motto is, Be Weirdly Wonderful! Embrace your disability and differences. She was born with a facial difference and lives with low vision,  anxiety and depression. North of Brisbane is home, with her youngest daughter, three cute cats and fluffy dog.

Jenny taught in a primary school for 25 years. She has published eight middle grade/YA novels on being different. Her latest, *Simon Sees*, is about a twelve-year-old boy who is diagnosed with Retinitis Pigmentosa. *Simon Sees* is endorsed by Guide Dogs Australia. All Jenny's novels aim to self-empower children to be themselves. Jenny's all-age short stories have been included in eighteen anthologies.

Jenny is heavily involved in volunteering with her local high school, Special Olympics, and Guide Dogs. She is also a mentor with the Queensland Writers Centre and runs Writing Friday at her local library. When she isn't volunteering or caring, Jenny plays with clay.

You can find Jenny at

jennywoolsey.com
Facebook @JennyWoolseyAuthor
Insta @jennywoolseyauthor

LILY MULHOLLAND is an Australian writer, singer-songwriter, actor and rapscallion. Lily loves to explore the role of women in society through a range of genres and media.

Her romance stories are grounded in the struggles everyone faces in finding a partner who doesn't complete them (as they are already a whole person) but who sees, hears and cherishes them and supports them in becoming their best selves. Like diamonds made under pressure, her heroines use their inner strength to overcome life's challenges, so they are ready to accept the love that is offered.

You can find Lily at

lilymulholland.com.au
Insta @lm_mulholland

ELIZABETH SPRATT was born in Sydney and has lived there her entire life. During the week she is a professional accountant, longing to find extra hours in the day to devote to her passion for creative writing. From a young age, Elizabeth  was always penning different stories. Over the past few years she decided to take the plunge and write her first novel. She is currently re-editing a second draft of a spy thriller and working on a new cosy mystery.

Elizabeth loves mystery and crime thrillers. She loves to travel to all parts of the world. With limited travel options post Covid she decided to combine travel and writing together and attended the 2021 and 2022 Rainforest Writers Retreat. She is thrilled to be part of the 2023 RWR Romance anthology. Her published stories, 'Tahitian Jewel' in *Charms of Love*, 'How Not to Host a Mystery Party' in *Got Game?* and 'Nothing Ever Happens in Anafi' in *Meanwhile Murder*.

AURA GOLD, a debut author, with a published short story 'Sleepover' found in RWR *Charms of Love*, also delves into memoir writing, poetry, song writing, and film.

A Drama prize winner at Sydney University, she embraces theatre while exploring the creative realm of filmmaking. Her journey inspires her memoir, and she finds solace in water when not creating.

KATE KELSEN is a writer, circus entertainer and world traveller, and takes a particular interest in exploring various human experiences and perspectives.

In 2023, Kate was selected in the Outback Writers Festival Short Story Competition. Her entry, a story about a dinner date in a small township in Kakadu, was published in the annual anthology.

In 2022, Kate received her first international writing recognition, selected as a Finalist in the 2022 Wild Atlantic Writing Awards. That same year, she was shortlisted for the 2022 SD Harvey Short Crime Story Award, and won the 2022 GenreCon Short Story Competition.

Kate's previous recognitions include the Grieve Writing Competition (2014 & 2015), and Reader's Digest 100 Word Short Story Competition.

She has been published in two previous Rainforest Writing Retreat anthologies, 'Undetected' in *Meanwhile Murder* (2021) and 'Delete World' in *Got Game?* (2022).

You can find Kate at

katekelsen.com

REVIEWS

Your words are as important to an author as an author's words are to you.

GOODREADS.COM

Please leave a review

AMAZON.COM.AU

Feed an author, leave a review. It takes five minutes and helps more than you can imagine.

ACKNOWLEDGEMENTS

RWR would like to thank Chris Radge (Christine Titheradge), Charmaine Clancy, Gina Pinto, for their hard work in assembling this anthology.

Likewise, thanks are also due to the RWR retreaters/authors, without their work there wouldn't be an anthology.

Big thanks to all the crew at the Self-Publishing Lab for everything you do. You can contact them at selfpublishinglab. com for a website setup and publishing needs.

And the biggest thanks to Charmaine who thought that a writing retreat would be a great idea and has run with it ever since.

CHARMS OF LOVE

Self-publishing Lab
Formerly BookCover

SELF-PUBLISHING AND MARKETING YOUR BOOK JUST GOT SIMPLER

selfpublishinglab.com

Online **Classroom**

The Lab is packed with in-depth, step-by-step practical video lessons, tools and resources on preparing, producing, publishing and promoting your book. PLUS the 24/7 community and coaching you need to ensure you achieve your full potential and goals.

Book **Creation**

Let us take care of these one-off tasks, so you can avoid any headaches. Our team is ready when you are. The Lab is an award-winning one-stop shop for creating and publishing a quality book with a team of professionals who care. Oh, and you'll have fun doing it too!

Book **Marketing & Coaching**

From Amazon Ads, building email lists to selling at tradeshows, the Lab has you covered. With courses, templates and our online community, all your questions can be answered with the support of the Lab team and other like-minded authors achieving their goals, just like you.

About the **Self-publishing Lab**

The Lab is an award-winning publishing destination helping thousands of writers avoid the traps in publishing and get started on the right foot.

With over 25 years in the publishing industry, Anthony and the team at the Self-publishing Lab continue to help authors become bestsellers, sell thousands of dollars worth of books online, at schools, workshops and to organisations.

Here's what makes the **Self-publishing Lab different**

 No contracts or exclusive agreements that sell your soul. You'll keep 100% royalties and control without it costing you an arm and a leg to publish your book.

 We show you how to use technology to sell more books while you sleep, even if you're a tech newbie.

 Have your book distributed and available for purchase online around the world, at bookstores and libraries in print and e-book.

....

Contact Us Today

 w: selfpublishinglab.com
e: support@selfpublishinglab.com

 PO BOX 187
Browns Plains, QLD
Australia, 4118

WANT TO WRITE A NOVEL?
DON'T KNOW WHERE TO START?

Join us at Australia's favourite writing retreat.

LEARN

Immersive workshops, mentoring & publishing tips from International best-selling authors and industry experts.

CONNECT

Find the support you need and new life-long friends who share your passion. Network, laugh and connect.

PUBLISH

Every year, RWR puts out a high-quality anthology only open to Retreaters for submissions.

SECURE YOUR SPOT!

Each year, sixty writers gather at the spectacular Australian rainforest. Many of our writers have gone ahead to publish their first works because of the ongoing support and guidance they receive. RWR can book out over six months ahead, so get in early and secure your place. Once you have become a Retreater, you'll also be invited to our private mastermind group, meet-ups, extra workshops and qualify to submit to our publications.

www.RainforestWritingRetreat.com

www.ingramcontent.com/pod-product-compliance
Lightning Source LLC
Chambersburg PA
CBHW030624120726
47904CB00006B/2019